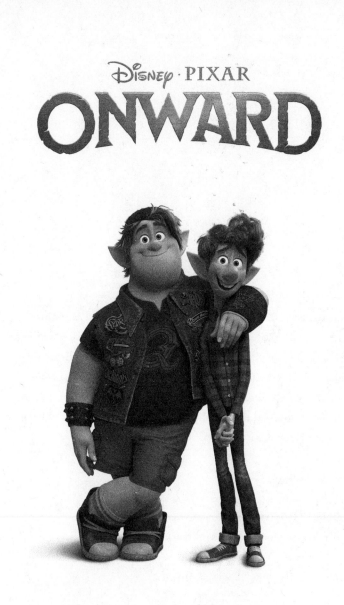

rhcbooks.com

ISBN 978-0-7364-4050-9 (hardcover)
ISBN 978-0-7364-3965-7 (paperback)

Printed in the United States of America

10 9 8 7 6 5 4 3 2 1

DISNEY · PIXAR
ONWARD

The Deluxe Junior Novelization

Adapted by Suzanne Francis

Random House New York

Prologue

Long, long ago, before smartphones, televisions, and even electricity, the world was very different. Sprites and unicorns soared across the sky as centaurs, satyrs, cyclops, elves, and merfolk frolicked below. The world was full of wonder. It was adventurous, exciting, and best of all . . . there was MAGIC!

During those wondrous days, wizards would cast spells, shouting incantations like *"Boombastia!"* and *"Flame Infernar!"* and *"Voltar Thundasir!"* Magic burst from their staffs with dazzling beams of light.

Those who mastered magic tackled unfathomable challenges. Skilled wizards could make objects float, create fire, or even assist a warrior on a quest by defeating terrible beasts, such as hydras and dragons!

Wizards didn't hesitate to help those in need, and everyone enjoyed what magic could do.

But it wasn't easy. Becoming a wizard required patience, practice, and persistence. And only those with the gift of magic could perform the spells. So with new technology, the world found simpler ways to get by. Instead of taking years to learn how to perform the Light Spell, even the lowliest elf could just flick a switch to turn on an electric light bulb. Or they could turn on a gas stove rather than conjure fire with magic. Eventually the students of wizardry tossed away their staffs, ready for the life of ease that technology made possible.

Soon everyone embraced toasters, gas fireplaces, buses, and cars, and became accustomed to all the conveniences of modern life. Sprites traveled for work by airplane instead of using their wings to fly. Centaurs drove instead of galloping across the land. Bored teens played video games or gazed at their smartphones instead of setting off on adventurous quests.

Thus, over time, magic faded away. . . .

1

The sun rose over the city of New Mushroomton as residents began their morning routines. Garbage trucks picked up trash along the suburban streets. Scavenging unicorns scattered as the trucks rolled past.

Ian Lightfoot, a shy, awkward elf, was inside his cozy mushroom home getting ready for school. His eyes landed on the calendar on his desk, and he focused on the date. It was circled, and on it he'd written 16TH B-DAY. He took a deep breath and headed downstairs with his head held high, ready to take on the day and hopeful that age sixteen would mark the beginning of a bright new chapter in his life.

Loud, pulsing music blared from the living room. Ian's mother, Laurel, was dressed in workout gear and exercising in front of the television. She followed along as a cyclops barked out commands: *"We're gonna get Warrior Z-Ninety fit! Let me hear you say 'I'm a mighty warrior!'"*

"Morning, Mom!" Ian called over the music. He repeated himself, but his mom still didn't hear him. The family's small pet dragon, Blazey, blasted into the room. Ian screamed as she tackled him to the ground and licked his face all over.

Finally noticing Ian trapped beneath the wiry dragon, Laurel grabbed a spray bottle and squirted the energetic pet with water.

"Blazey, down! Bad dragon! Back to your lair!" she scolded. Blazey blew a small puff of fire at her before trotting off.

When Ian got back on his feet, Laurel attacked him with kisses. "HAPPY BIRTHDAY, MR. ADULT MAN!" she squealed.

"Ugh, no, Mom!" Ian said, laughing as he squirmed away. "Ah, gross."

"Hey, buddy, don't wipe off my kisses—" She stepped back and gazed at him.

"What?" he asked.

"You're wearing your dad's sweatshirt."

"Oh, you know. Finally fits."

"Oh, my little chubby cheeks is all grown up," Laurel cooed, moving toward him again.

"Okay, okay, Mom! I gotta eat something before school," Ian said, heading toward the kitchen.

Laurel followed behind. "Oh, we don't have much food. I still have to go to the grocery store—" Ian reached toward a covered platter inside the refrigerator and Laurel smacked his hand. "Hands off, mister! Those are for your party tonight."

Ian grabbed the milk from the fridge and closed the door. "It's not a party, Mom; it's just us." He pulled the last box of cereal out of the cabinet and emptied what little was left into a bowl.

"Well, you could invite those kids from your science class. You said they seemed pretty rockin'." She opened a container of protein powder.

"I'm pretty sure I didn't say it like that," Ian replied, "and besides, I don't even know them."

"Well, your birthday is a day to try new things, be the new you!" Laurel poured the powder into a blender, added water, secured the top, and hit the power button. It roared to life with a deafening

WHIRRRR. She screamed over the noise. "SPEAKING OF TRYING NEW THINGS, DID YOU SIGN UP FOR DRIVING PRACTICE?"

"NO!" shouted Ian as Laurel turned off the blender. "No," he repeated, quietly this time.

Laurel poured her protein shake into a glass. "I know you're a little scared to drive, sweetie-pie, but—"

Ian let out a nervous giggle. "I'm not scared, Mom." He gestured to a board game called Quests of Yore, set up on the kitchen table. Small pewter figurines, dice, and cards had been carefully placed across the board. "I'm gonna move Barley's game."

"Okay, but you know how he gets when someone touches that board."

As Ian approached the kitchen table, he tripped on a plastic weapon on the floor and nearly dropped his cereal. He caught himself, put the bowl down, and reached for one of the figurines. "Well, he's gotta learn to clean up his toys—"

Ian screamed as a thick arm suddenly wrapped around his neck and a booming voice yelled, "HALT!"

2

Ian was pulled into the hulking chest of his older brother, Barley. "Doth my brother dare disrupt an active campaign?" said Barley. He wrestled Ian away from the game, knocking the bowl of cereal to the floor.

"Oh, come on!" groaned Ian.

"You know, Ian, in the days of old, a boy of sixteen would have his strength tested in the Swamps of Despair," said Barley, his arm still wrapped tightly around Ian.

"I'm not testing anything—just let me go!" Ian said, struggling.

"Let him go," ordered Laurel.

Barley smiled and released him. "Okay, but I know

you're stronger than that. There's a mighty warrior inside you. You just gotta let him out. Right, Mom?"

Barley turned to Laurel and pounced, instantly putting her in the same chokehold. She laughed as she fought back, then recoiled. "Barley, you stink! When was the last time you showered?" They playfully wrestled as Blazey ran back into the room and roared and leapt around them excitedly. In the midst of the chaos, Ian cleaned up his scattered cereal.

"If you tried a little harder, you actually could probably wiggle out of this . . . ," said Barley.

Laurel smirked and flipped Barley onto his back, knocking the air right out of him.

"See?" said Barley, catching his breath. "Mom knows how to let out her inner warrior." Still on his back, Barley reached up for a high five.

"Thank you. Now take out the trash," said Laurel, helping him up.

Barley grabbed the bag of garbage and carried it through the back door. As soon as he stepped outside, he heard the distinct sounds of a police radio. "Officer Bronco," he groaned.

A mustachioed centaur cop wearing mirrored aviator sunglasses stepped from the shadows. "Barley,

Barley, Barley," said Officer Colt Bronco, shaking his head. "Every time the city tries to tear down an old piece of rubble, I gotta drag my rear end out here and deal with you."

"I don't know what you're talking about," said Barley.

"Oh, really?" said Colt. He took out his phone and played a streaming video.

The footage showed Barley clinging to an ancient fountain. *"I won't let you tear down this fountain!"* he exclaimed. A crowd of construction workers and cops yelled at him as he continued to shout, *"Ancient warriors on grand quests drank from its flowing waters!"*

Colt turned off his phone and looked at Barley with his eyebrows raised.

Laurel, who had been standing in the doorway long enough to see the video, sighed. "Barley."

"They are destroying this town's past!" he exclaimed.

"And last night someone destroyed their bulldozer," said Colt.

Barley shrugged.

Laurel turned to Colt with another sigh. "Ugh. Well, come on in, rest your haunches for a minute."

"Thank you, hon," Colt said. He entered the house

and gave Laurel a kiss. Barley and Ian winced at the sight. Their mom having a boyfriend was gross.

Colt approached Ian and grinned. "Hey there, birthday boy. . . . So, ya workin' hard, or hardly workin'?" He punched Ian on the shoulder a little too hard and let out a loud horsey laugh.

"I'm just . . . making toast," said Ian as he opened a jar of jam.

Laurel narrowed her eyes at her older son. "I'm serious, Barley. You need to start thinking less about the past and more about your future."

Colt turned and accidentally knocked the toast out of Ian's hand with his tail. It fell to the floor, jam-side down. Before Ian could react, Blazey whipped by and snatched it up. Ian sighed and started making himself another piece of toast.

"She's right," said Colt. "You can't spend all day playing your board game." He plopped his lower, horse half into a chair at the kitchen table with a grunt. The pewter figurines on the board rattled and fell over.

Barley gasped. "Uh, Quests of Yore isn't just a board game. It's a historically based role-playing scenario," he said, quickly setting the pieces back in place. "Did you know in the old days, centaurs could run seventy miles an hour?"

"I own a vehicle. Don't need to run," said Colt, unimpressed.

Barley turned to his brother. "Well, Ian, you could definitely learn a lot from Quests of Yore. You want to play?"

"I don't," answered Ian.

"You could be a crafty rogue, or . . . Ooh, I know! You can be a wizard." Barley pushed a pewter wizard onto Ian's shoulder and said in a mysterious deep voice, "I shall cast a spell on thee!"

"Hey, careful of Dad's sweatshirt," said Ian, eyeing the wizard on his shoulder.

"I don't even remember Dad wearing that sweatshirt," said Barley.

"Well, you do only have, like, two memories of him."

"No! I've got three. I remember his beard was scratchy, he had a goofy laugh, and I used to play—"

"Drums on his feet," Ian said along with him. They had talked about it a thousand times.

"I used to go . . . ," said Barley, and hummed "Shave and a Haircut." When he got to the last two beats, he stopped humming and blew two raspberries. Then he accidentally knocked Ian's toast off the counter. Ian lunged for it, but it fell on the floor. As Barley picked up the bread, his spiked wrist cuff bracelet caught on the seam of Ian's sweatshirt and snagged it.

Ian gasped.

Barley looked down at the snag. "It's okay! You just gotta pull it!" He yanked his arm to break off the thread and it unraveled even more, causing the seam to open.

"Barley!" shouted Laurel, hurrying over to cut the thread.

Ian stared at his brother, holding in his frustration. He took a deep breath. "You know what, I'm just gonna get some food on the way to school."

"I'll sew that later tonight, okay?" said Laurel.

Barley jumped to his feet, slapped on a helmet, and picked up a sword. "Wait! By the laws of Yore, I must dub thee a man today! Kneel before me."

"Oh, that's okay . . . I gotta get going!" said Ian, eager to get out of the house and as far from Barley as possible.

"All right, well, I'll pick you up later and we'll perform the ceremony at school!"

"NO! No, no, no, no, no. Don't do that. Okay, bye!" said Ian, quickly backing out the door.

Ready for a fresh start to his day, Ian headed to his favorite fast-food restaurant. As he sat down to wait for his order, an elf named Gaxton approached.

"Hey! Go Griffins!" said Gaxton.

"What?" asked Ian, perplexed.

Gaxton pointed to the logo on Ian's sweatshirt. "You go to Willowdale College?" He handed his son a receipt and sent him to the counter to wait for their food.

"Oh, no," answered Ian. "This was my dad's." He pointed to where LIGHTFOOT was embroidered on it.

"Lightfoot? Wilden Lightfoot?"

"Yeah!" said Ian, excited to meet someone who had known his father. It was just the thing he needed to turn his morning around.

"You're kidding! I went to college with him!" said Gaxton, beaming. His smile faded. "Yeah. Boy, I was so sorry to hear that he passed away."

Ian nodded and thanked him.

"You know, your dad was a great guy!" Gaxton continued. "So confident. When he came into a room, people noticed." He laughed as he recalled. "The man wore the ugliest purple socks, every single day."

Ian laughed, too. "What? Why?"

"Hey, that's exactly what we asked," said Gaxton. "But he was just bold. I always wished I had a little bit of that in me."

"Yeah. Wow. I've never heard any of this about him before," said Ian. "Do you remember—"

Just then, Gaxton's son interrupted, calling to his dad from the counter and holding up a bag of food.

Gaxton apologized as he gestured toward his son. "Gotta get this guy off to school." He held out his hand. "Hey, it was nice meeting you!"

"Yeah, you too," said Ian, shaking his hand.

Gaxton took off, and Ian waited for a moment, lost in thought. Every single thing he knew about his father was what other people had told him. Discovering something new about his dad's past made his mind race.

A plan began to form in Ian's mind. He knew what he had to do to kick-start his new year. After picking up his breakfast, he hurried off to school with a spring in his step.

3

Ian sat outside New Mushroomton High School writing his plan in a notebook. At the top of the page, he wrote *NEW ME*. Below it, he added a list:

Speak up more
Learn to drive
Invite people to party
Be like Dad

The bell rang and Ian snapped the notebook shut and headed inside.

Moments later, he walked into a classroom as the teacher called attendance. A large troll named Gorgamon sat in the desk behind his. He wore flip-flops and propped his giant, gross feet on Ian's seat, like he did every day. Ian thought about the first thing on his list: *Speak up more.* He took a deep breath.

"Hey, uh, Gorgamon . . . um, would you mind not putting your feet on my chair today?" he said.

"Sorry, dude, gotta keep 'em elevated," said Gorgamon. "Gets the blood flowing to my brain."

"It just makes it a little hard for me to fit in there—" started Ian.

"Well, if I don't have good blood flow, I can't concentrate on my schoolwork. You don't want me to do bad in school, do you?" Gorgamon interrupted.

"Uh . . . no," Ian said with an awkward laugh. He couldn't help feeling a little disappointed in himself as, just like always, he scooted up to the edge of his seat, making room for Gorgamon's disgusting feet.

Later that afternoon, a goblin teacher stood next to a small car with a DRIVER'S ED sign on the roof. When she asked if any of the students wanted to volunteer to take the first road test, a nervous Ian forced himself to raise his hand.

Moments later, he was driving with the instructor

sitting in the passenger seat and two other students in the back.

"A left here," the instructor said.

Ian signaled and turned.

"Now take this on-ramp to the expressway."

"Okay, yeah," said Ian, his voice slightly trembling. "I'm super ready for that." His forced smile faded as he got closer to the expressway traffic. "It's nice and . . . fast."

"Just merge into traffic," said the instructor.

"Just any minute . . . ," said Ian, growing more and more nervous.

"Merge into traffic!" yelled the instructor. "MERGE INTO TRAFFIC!"

"I'm not ready!" Ian shrieked. The instructor ordered him to pull over, and he veered off the expressway, stopping on the shoulder. He couldn't believe it—he had failed again!

+ .✦.✦. ☾ ✦.✦.+

When the last bell finally rang, students poured out of the school to hang out and chat on the front lawn.

Ian stood nearby quietly talking to himself.

"Oh, hey! What's up, dudes? I'm having a party tonight and was wondering if you want to come over and get down on some cake. . . ." His smile dropped. "That's not something anyone says." He looked at his palm, reviewing the words he'd written there. He used a pen to cross out "dudes" and changed it to "gang."

"Okay, don't say 'dudes,'" he said. "Gang? What's up, gang?" It still wasn't quite right, so he tried again in a friendly tone. "What's up, gang?"

He exhaled and approached a group from his science class. He was determined to accomplish an item from his list by inviting some people to his birthday celebration.

"Hey, what's up, gang?" he asked, trying to sound confident.

They turned and faced him. "Oh, hey . . . Ian, right?" said an elf named Sadalia.

Ian was surprised. "Oh, I didn't know you knew my . . ." He looked down at his palm and saw that the words were smeared from his sweat. "Uh, anyway. If you like parties, then I was gonna do a party."

"What?" asked Sadalia.

"What I was trying to say is if you're not doing

anything tonight—but I'm sure you probably are doing something tonight—and you like cake like I like cake, I've got a cake . . . at my house."

The group looked at each other, a bit confused.

"Are you inviting us to a party?" asked Sadalia.

"That's the one," said Ian, relieved that she understood what he was trying to say.

"Oh, yeah! We don't have any plans," she said, glancing at the group.

The others agreed and Ian looked up, completely shocked by their response.

"Really? I guess we can just take the bus over to my house—"

Just then, the sound of fantasy metal music and a backfiring engine caused him to pause. Everyone but Ian looked to see the source of the noise as an old van sputtered up to the curb, a large Pegasus painted on the side. Lightning bolts flashed around the winged horse as it reared up on its hind legs.

"Oh, no, no, no, no, no," Ian chanted quietly, refusing to turn around.

"Ha! Is that the birthday boy I see?" called Barley, hanging out the driver's-side window. "Behold! Your chariot awaits!"

The group looked at Ian. "Do you know that guy?" asked a cyclops named Althea.

"Sir Iandore of Lightfoot!" Barley shouted from the window.

"Seems like he's talking to you," added Althea.

"HEY, IAN!" Barley yelled while honking the loud, distorted horn.

Finally, Ian turned around. "Hey, Barley. . . . Yeah, we're actually gonna take the bus."

"The bus? Nay! I will give you and your companions transport upon Guinevere!"

"Um, who's Guinevere?" asked a satyr named Parthenope.

"My mighty steed!" said Barley. He proudly smacked the old van, causing a bumper to fall off. "Oops, that's embarrassing! That's okay, girl. We'll patch you back up." Barley stepped out of the van holding a thick roll of duct tape. He ripped off a few long pieces of tape and used them to reattach the bumper. As he bent over to secure it, his pants sagged, showing the top of his backside. A couple of the kids giggled.

Ian groaned and slapped his hand over his face,

mortified. He turned to the group. "He's just joking around."

They looked at Ian and frowned. He had unknowingly wiped some of the sweaty ink off his hand onto his cheek.

"You've got something on your face," said Sadalia.

Ian wiped the clean side of his face, smearing more ink across it.

"Oh, no. You just—oh! Right," said Sadalia.

As Ian wiped, he spread more ink. Finally, he looked down at his hand and realized what had happened. "Oh!" he said. "Uh . . . you know what? I just remembered that my birthday is, uh . . . canceled."

"What?" asked Althea.

"I mean, the party," said Ian. "It was never actually happening. It was just this huge misunderstanding, so I gotta go. Okay, bye!"

The group watched, confused, as Ian raced off and hopped into the van. As he tried to sit, Barley chuckled and scooped up a pile of parking tickets from the passenger seat.

"Whoops," said Barley. "Let me just file those." He grabbed the tickets and shoved them into the glove box. Then he looked over at Ian and gasped. "Hey! Did those kids write on your face?" He licked his thumb and started to rub it off. "Here, I'll get it."

Ian pushed Barley's hand away. "Can we please just go home?"

"Okay, we'll perform your birthday ceremony later," said Barley. "Then you'll be ready for adulthood and its gauntlet of challenges!" Barley looked out the window as he babbled on. "You know, in ancient times, you celebrated your day of birth with a solemn quest."

Ian slumped in his seat, feeling like a complete failure and trying to tune Barley out. The last thing he wanted to hear was one of his brother's speeches about ancient times. As they drove away, the dragon mascot painted on the side of the school gym caught Ian's eye. Its goofy grin and big thumbs-up made him feel even worse.

Back in his room, Ian sat at his desk and pulled out his "New Me" list. Clicking his pen, he crossed off the first three items:

~~Speak up more~~
~~Learn to drive~~
~~Invite people to party~~

He paused a moment before striking a line through the last one:

~~Be like Dad~~

The setting sun gave his room a dark purple glow. It seemed to fit his gloomy mood. He sighed, crumpled up the list, and tossed it into the trash.

Family photos covered his bulletin board, and his eyes fell on a photo taken shortly before he was born. His father posed with three-year-old Barley alongside Laurel, who was pregnant with Ian at the time. The three of them smiled, looking incredibly happy together. He moved his attention to the photo beside it, taken a few months later. There were Laurel, three-year-old Barley, and Ian as a baby. The space where his father should have been was painfully empty.

He pulled a cassette tape labeled DAD out of its place in his desk drawer and popped it into a player. Scratchy audio came through the tiny speakers. He listened intently to a conversation between his parents from years ago, recorded before he was born.

"Will, you're not gonna get that thing working," said young Laurel.

"I think I've got it," said his dad. Ian could hear the sounds of his father messing with the recorder.

"I'm gonna watch from over here when it blows up," Laurel said, stepping away.

"Hello? Hello?" said Dad's voice, clear as a bell.

The audio of Laurel's voice drifted into the

background. *"I'll bet good money you can't get it to work,"* she said.

"Oh, is that right?" said Dad. Ian could hear his smile.

"Yup," she said. *"But you're doing a good job of making it look like you know what you're doing."*

"Well, I'm trying to," said Dad with a laugh.

Laurel, her voice faint, asked, *"Did you check if it had batteries?"* Dad laughed even louder and she added, *"No, I'm serious."*

"I know."

"So is it really working?" asked Laurel, still far from the machine.

"Well, let's find out." There was a brief moment of silence before Dad said, *"Okay. Bye."*

The tape ended and Ian rewound it and played it again. But this time, he talked back to the recording in the places where Laurel's voice could barely be heard. It was the only way he could feel like he was having some version of a conversation with his father. He knew it was a little strange, but it brought him a tiny bit of comfort.

"Hi, Dad," said Ian, staring at his father's photo.

Dad's voice on the recording said, *"Hello? Hello?"*

"It's me, Ian."

"Oh, is that right?"

"Yeah. Did you have a good day?" asked Ian.

"Well, I'm trying to."

"Yeah, me too. Although I could clearly use some help." There was laughter on the recording before Ian added, "I sure do wish I could spend a day with you sometime."

"I know."

"Yeah, there are so many things we could do. I bet it'd be really fun!" said Ian.

"Well, let's find out."

"Yeah, I mean, I'd love to! We could, uh—"

Dad's recorded voice cut Ian off. *"Okay. Bye."*

"Yeah," said Ian sadly. "Bye."

Ian stopped the tape and leaned back, lost in his thoughts. It was odd missing someone he had never met, but he thought about his father all the time. And special days, like birthdays, were especially difficult. He sighed, feeling an emptiness that he was sure could never be filled.

He went downstairs to fix his torn sweatshirt.

When Laurel saw him starting to sew, she said, "Honey, I was going to do that."

"That's okay," he replied.

Laurel smiled as she watched him. "Wow, you must have been taught by some kind of sewing master."

"Yeah, a very humble sewing master," said Ian with a smirk.

When he'd finished the last few stitches, he held the thread out for Laurel to snip with the scissors.

Ian touched the word stitched onto the front of the hoodie: LIGHTFOOT.

"What was Dad like when he was my age?" he asked. "Was he always super confident?"

"Oh, no," said Laurel. "It took him a while to find out who he was."

"I wish I'd met him," said Ian.

"Oh, me too," said Laurel, her voice full of longing. "But hey, you know, when your dad got sick, he fought so hard . . . because he wanted to meet you more than anything." Laurel looked lovingly at her son, then became upbeat. "You know what—I have something for you. I was going to wait until after cake, but . . . I think you've waited long enough."

"What is it?" asked Ian.

"It's a gift . . . from your dad."

. ⚔. ᶜC ✦.⁺.

Moments later, Ian hurried up the stairs with Barley behind him.

"What do you mean it's from Dad?" asked Barley.

"I don't know!" said Ian. "Mom said it was for both of us."

Barley and Ian watched with anticipation as Laurel climbed down the attic ladder carrying a long item wrapped in canvas.

"He just said to give you this when you were both over sixteen," explained Laurel. "I have no idea what it is."

They rushed into Ian's room, and Laurel set the gift down on the bed.

"Well . . . open it!" she said, looking at Ian.

He pulled back the cloth to reveal a wooden staff.

Barley gasped. "NO WAY!" He picked it up in amazement. "It's a wizard staff! DAD WAS A WIZARD!"

"What?" asked Ian.

Laurel shook her head. "Hold on—your Dad was

an accountant. I mean, he got interested in a lot of strange things when he got sick, but—"

Ian found a letter and read it aloud:

Dear Ian and Barley:

Long ago, the world was full of wonder! It was adventurous, exciting, and best of all . . . there was magic. And that magic helped all in need. But it wasn't easy to master. And so the world found a simpler way to get by. Over time, magic faded away, but I hope there's a little magic left . . . in you. And so I wrote this spell so I could see for myself who my boys grew up to be.

Ian looked at the second page of the letter and read the bold words across the top: "'Visitation Spell'?"

Barley snatched the page from Ian and examined it. Beneath its title was an illustration of a wizard staff with a beam of light shooting from it, forming the shape of a person.

"I don't believe this," whispered Barley. "This spell brings him back. For one whole day, Dad will be back!"

Ian was confused, but he couldn't help feeling excited. "Back? Like back to life? That's not possible."

Barley held up the staff. "It is with this."

"I'm gonna meet Dad?" said Ian, shocked.

Barley nodded as Laurel grabbed the letter.

"Oh, Will, you wonderful nut," she said. "What *is* this?"

Barley dug through the canvas. "Now, a spell this powerful needs an assist element. For this to work, Dad would've had to find a . . ." He removed a sparkling orange stone from the package and held it up to the light. "Phoenix Gem! Wow. There are only a few of these left." He carefully slid the gem into an open space at the very top of the staff.

"Wait, hold on—is this dangerous?" asked Laurel.

Barley held out the staff and the spell, suddenly very serious. "We're about to find out."

Everyone waited in suspense. . . . Then Barley screamed, causing Ian and Laurel to jump with fright.

"What!" Laurel asked.

"Splinter," Barley said, sucking on his finger. He shook it off and struck a dramatic pose in the center of the bedroom. Then he read the spell:

Only once is all we get; grant me this rebirth.
Till tomorrow's sun has set, one day to walk the earth!

He braced himself, ready for the magic to begin . . . but . . . nothing happened.

Ian and Laurel stared at Barley.

"Hold on, I was just gripping it wrong," Barley said. He adjusted his hands and refocused, reciting the spell again, a bit louder. But still, nothing happened.

Determined, Barley tried the spell again and again. And again.

Finally, Laurel stopped him. He leaned the staff against Ian's desk and plopped onto the bed beside them. Laurel put her hand on Barley's shoulder and the three of them sat silently for a moment, sharing sadness and longing for the man they missed so much.

Laurel picked up the spell. "I'm sorry you guys don't have your dad here, but this shows just how much he wanted to see you both. So much that he'd try anything. That's still a pretty special gift," she said, her voice cracking with emotion.

Barley sighed and left without a word.

Laurel turned to Ian. "Hey, want to come with me to pick up your cake?"

"That's okay. Thanks, Mom."

Laurel walked toward the door and paused before leaving, wishing she could make it all better. She quietly headed down the stairs and off to the bakery.

Ian sat on his bed. He picked up the spell and examined it for a moment before reading it aloud. "*'Only once is all we get; grant me this rebirth . . .'*" With those words, something strange started to happen!

5

As the beginning of the spell passed Ian's lips, the wooden staff glowed with light! He continued to read it aloud, and the staff began to tremble and the light grew brighter. Suddenly, it seemed as though all the air was sucked out of the room, and objects, including the staff, began to rise toward the ceiling! As the staff began to fall, Ian caught it. He stood holding it, and finished the spell. A beam of light blasted from the top of the staff!

Hearing the ruckus, Barley rushed in. "Hey, man. What are you doing in here— Holy Tooth of Zadar!" He couldn't believe his eyes. "How did you—"

"I don't know, it just started!" shouted Ian, struggling to hold the staff as his books, clothes, and furniture swirled around him. It was like being in a chaotic tornado!

Blazey poked her head in the doorway for a quick moment, then raced away, spooked. Ian gripped the staff with all his might as it shook more and more. The beam of light sent its magic onto the floor and began generating a pair of men's dress shoes!

"Whoa, feet!" exclaimed Barley.

Ian gasped as bright purple socks appeared above the shoes. The spell was working—it was bringing back their father!

As the light moved upward, pants started to materialize, and it continued all the way up to a belt! Then a shirt began to form, one button at a time.

The gem rose out of the staff and spun wildly as the light grew brighter and brighter. It became more difficult for Ian to hold on to the staff. Suddenly, Dad's body shrank back down to the waist. Something wasn't right.

"Hang on, I can help!" shouted Barley, rushing toward Ian.

Ian backed away. "BARLEY, NO!"

The light exploded and the gem burst into a million pieces! The force of it shot Ian and Barley across the room and shattered the window. The shards disintegrated to dust.

Barley helped Ian up and they both looked around the messy room, desperately searching for their father.

A sudden rustling behind a pile of clothes in the closet got the boys' attention. A pair of legs in khaki pants and dress shoes kicked out!

"Dad?" said Ian.

The legs stood to reveal . . . no upper half! Ian and Barley screamed.

"He's just legs!" exclaimed Barley. "There's no top part. I definitely remember Dad having a top part!"

Ian and Barley watched, horrified, as Dad's legs walked around the room.

"Oh, what did I do?" said Ian, panicking. "This is horrible!" He paced, trying to calm himself, then kneeled in an attempt to talk to the pants. "Hello?" He reached out and ran his hand through the area of the missing torso.

One of Dad's feet began tapping around, as if it was trying to get a feel for the space. Ian and Barley watched the legs move around the room like a toddler learning to walk.

"It's really him," said Barley.

The boys watched, amazed. Then Dad ran into a wall, interrupting the moment of wonder. He stopped and searched with his foot again, clearly confused and lost.

"DAD! You are in your house!" shouted Barley.

Dad bumped into a dresser and a bunch of books fell on top of him, knocking him down. The boys raced over and helped him stand.

"Ah, he can't hear us," said Ian.

Barley walked over to Dad's legs and slowly began to tap on his foot.

Ian watched curiously. "What are you doing?"

Barley hummed the first five beats of "Shave and a Haircut." Dad's legs leapt back. Dad tapped the final two notes of the song and touched Barley's feet with his foot, patting them gently.

Barley's face lit up. "That's right, Dad. It's me, Barley." Dad felt around to find Ian's foot and gave it a tap. "Yeah, that's Ian."

"Hi . . . Dad," Ian said softly. He put his hand on Dad's foot, wishing he could give him a hug. "Oh . . . I messed this whole thing up, and now he's gonna be legs forever!"

Barley looked at the spell. "Well, not . . . forever. The spell only lasts one day. At sunset tomorrow, he'll disappear and we'll never be able to bring him back again." He showed Ian two illustrations: the first was of a man standing by the sun, and the second depicted the sun setting and the man vanishing.

Ian sighed. "Okay, okay, okay. Twenty-four hours . . . that doesn't give us much time, but—" He looked at his phone, only to see that it had broken in the chaos of the magic. He tossed it aside and programmed his watch to count down twenty-four hours. "We'll just have to do the spell again."

"You mean *you* have to," said Barley. He grabbed Ian and pulled him into a playful headlock. "A person can only do magic if they have the gift. And my little brother has the magic gift!"

Ian pushed him away. "But I couldn't even finish the spell."

"Well, you're gonna have plenty of time to practice. Because we have to find another Phoenix Gem."

Barley pulled out his Quests of Yore cards and began flipping through them. "Aha!" he said, finding what he was looking for. "We'll start at the place where all quests begin. . . ." Barley showed Ian a card with a picture of an old tavern on it that read THE PLACE WHERE ALL QUESTS BEGIN. "The Manticore's Tavern! It's run by a fearless adventurer. She knows where to find any kind of gem, talisman, totem . . ."

Ian frowned. "Barley, this is for a game."

"Based on real life!"

"But how do we know this tavern is still there?"

"It's there," said Barley. "Look, my years of training have prepared me for this very moment. And I'm telling you . . . this is the only way to find a Phoenix Gem." Barley held up a Phoenix Gem card. "Trust me."

Ian looked over at Dad's legs sitting in his desk chair and sighed. He knew he had no choice but to go with Barley's idea. "Whatever it takes, I am gonna meet my dad."

Barley smiled from ear to ear, more than ready for an adventure. "You hear that, Dad? We're going on a quest!"

6

Barley climbed into Guinevere's driver's seat, while Dad and Ian sat in the spacious back part of the van. Barley turned the key in the ignition. The engine strained, trying to start. "Come on, Guinevere," he said, patting the dashboard.

"Maybe we should just take the bus," said Ian.

"She's fine," said Barley. Then he grabbed a cassette tape labeled QUEST MIX and popped it into the stereo. Dramatic music played as Barley shouted, "H'YAH!" The van jerked forward, backfired, and spit puffs of black smoke as it headed off.

It wasn't long before they were driving through the city and past a road sign that read LEAVING NEW MUSHROOMTON. As Barley slowed to pay the troll working the tollbooth, Ian talked to Dad.

"Anyway, it's like this award for math," he said. "But I'll show you when we get back home."

"Hey, what are you two Chatty Charlies up to back there?" Barley asked, looking at them in the rearview mirror.

"You know, I felt weird talking to Dad without a top half, so . . . ta-da!" Ian moved aside to reveal that he had stuffed some clothing and attached it to the pants to make a mock upper body and head! He had even fastened on a pair of sunglasses to make it look like Dad had eyes.

Barley thought it was great. "Dad, you look just like I remember. Hey, don't worry—we'll have the rest of you here before you know it. And then first thing I'm gonna do is introduce you to Guinevere. Rebuilt this old girl myself, from the lug nuts to the air-conditioning." He flipped a switch, and out blasted a gust of air.

Ian had to fight against its power to climb into the passenger seat, where he quickly turned it off. "Showing Dad your van? That's your whole list?"

"What list?"

"Oh . . . ," Ian said, regretting that he'd said

anything. "I'm just working on a list of things I want to do with Dad. You know, play catch, take a walk, driving lesson, share my whole life story with him."

Barley nodded. "That's cool." Then he reached down and picked up his Quests of Yore book. "Oh, but before you cast Dad's spell again, you're gonna have to practice your magic." He tossed the book to Ian.

"This book is for a game," said Ian, still having a hard time buying into Barley's rationale.

"I told you, everything in Quests of Yore is historically accurate! Even the spells. So start practicing, young sorcerer!"

Ian opened the book to a random page. "Okay, Dad," he said. "Let's try some magic."

+ . ⊁ + . ᶜ C ⁺ . ⁺ . ₊

Back in New Mushroomton, Laurel returned home with Ian's cake. She went up to his room to check on him and frowned when she saw a note taped to his door.

Back soon with a MIND-BLOWING surprise!

She stepped inside and gasped at the mess. Blazey sniffed around the desk and Laurel spotted the two Quests of Yore game cards: the Phoenix Gem and the Manticore's Tavern. She picked up the Manticore's Tavern card.

She rushed downstairs, grabbed her car keys, and hurried out.

✦ ✦ ☾ ✦ ✦

As Barley continued to drive, Ian sat in the back of the van, pointing the staff at an empty can of energy drink.

"Aloft Elevar," he said. A small spark ignited above the can. *"Aloft Elevar,"* he repeated, causing another small spark. "I can't get this Levitation Spell to work. Maybe I should try something else, like . . ." He flipped through the pages of the book. "Arcane Lightning?"

Barley chuckled with a snort. "Yeah, like a level-one mage could bust out the hardest spell in the enchanter's guidebook. Maybe we should stick with the easy ones."

"Well, it's not working," said Ian. "Am I saying it wrong?"

"You said it right. It's just, for any spell to work, you have to speak from your Heart's Fire."

"My what?" asked Ian.

"Your Heart's Fire. You must speak with passion. Don't hold back."

Ian gave him a doubtful look before trying again. *"Aloft Elevar!"* Another small spark flickered around the can.

"No, like—*Aloft Elevar!*" said Barley with great gusto.

Ian repeated the magic words, a bit louder.

"No, from your Heart's Fire!" insisted Barley.

"ALOFT ELEVAR!" yelled Ian.

"DON'T HOLD BACK!"

Ian yelled the spell louder.

"HEART'S FIRE!" Barley shouted.

Ian tossed the staff in anger. "STOP SAYING HEART'S FIRE!" He motioned to their father's legs. "I'm clearly not good at this!" Then he moved to sit next to Dad.

"Hey, it was a good start," Barley said gently.

Feeling defeated, Ian leaned back and put his feet up. Dad imitated his movements, putting his feet up, too. Ian couldn't help feeling a little less annoyed.

Just then, Barley gasped as he noticed something ahead. "Oh! Gather your courage—we've arrived. The Manticore's Tavern."

Ian looked out the window. The old tavern looked exactly like the one on the card! Suddenly, he felt hopeful. "Wow, it *is* still here."

Barley parked the van and they walked toward the building. Since Dad couldn't see where he was going, they attached Blazey's leash to one of his belt loops. Ian tugged on it, steering him in the right direction.

Before entering, Barley paused. "All right, listen. First, let me do the talking. Secondly, it's crucial we show the fearless Manticore the respect she deserves, or she will, thirdly, not give us a map to a Phoenix Gem."

"Whoa, whoa, wait. The map? I thought she had a Phoenix Gem!" said Ian.

Barley giggled. "You're so cute." He turned to Dad. "Hear that, Dad? He's a smart kid. He just doesn't know how quests work."

"Well, is there anything else you're forgetting to tell me?" asked Ian.

"Nope," said Barley.

And with that, Barley opened the oversized, ornate wooden door. Ian was stunned by what he saw inside.

7

The Manticore's Tavern was a magic-themed family restaurant! It was packed with families. Kids were playing games, coloring children's menus, and eating out of miniature cauldrons.

Barley anticipated Ian's doubts. "Okay, so the tavern has changed a little over the years, but the Manticore is still the real deal." He marched up to the hostess and bowed. "Madame, I request an audience with the Manticore!"

"But of course, m'lord," said the hostess. She turned and called, "Oh, Manticore!" Then she blew into a silly-looking plastic horn.

Another employee, dressed in a large, adorable plush Manticore costume, leapt over to them. It let out a chuckle and gave Ian a big hug.

Barley pushed the mascot away from Ian, irritated. "No, no, the real Manticore! The fearless adventurer!"

The mascot rubbed its giant eyes dramatically, pretending to cry.

"Oh, you mean Corey? She's over there," answered the hostess.

The kitchen doors burst open. A frantic Manticore struggled as she balanced plates on her hands and her scorpion tail. "QUICK, SOMEBODY HELP ME!" she said. "These griffin nuggets were supposed to go out minutes ago!" Various servers grabbed plates from her as they rushed by.

Ian stared at the Manticore, who was dressed in a restaurant uniform and wearing glasses. "That's the Manticore?" She wasn't what he'd imagined at all.

Barley got down on one knee and looked up at her with admiration and respect.

"O great and powerful Manticore!" he said.

"Whoa, sir! You're right in the hot zone," she said.

Barley cautiously followed behind, trying to get her attention. "Your Fearlessness?" he said. "My brother and I seek a map . . . to a Phoenix Gem."

The Manticore hurried over to the podium by the

front door and dug around on the shelf. "Oh, uh, well, you've come to the right tavern. I have the parchment you desire right here! BEHOLD!" She handed them a children's menu, which said FIND THE PHOENIX GEM!

"Oh . . . that's a children's menu," said Ian.

"Isn't that fun? They're all based on my old maps," she said. "Oh, uh, the great Manticore sends you on your adventure with a hero's blessing." She stuffed a small package into Ian's hands. "And here are some crayons."

"That's very amusing, Your Dominance, but might you have the real map?" asked Barley.

The Manticore gestured to a wall of swords, shields, and rolled-up scrolls as she continued to hurry about. "Uh . . . yeah, it's over there."

Barley and Ian saw a plaque under one scroll that read PHOENIX GEM. Barley excitedly reached for the scroll, but the Manticore grabbed it from him.

"Whoa, whoa, whoa! What are you doing? You can't take this," she said.

"We have to," said Barley. Then he lifted Dad's fake upper body to reveal the legs.

The Manticore gasped. "What is that!"

Ian tried to explain. "It's our dad. We have a chance to meet him, but—"

Barley stepped in front of Ian. "Buuuuut . . . we can't do that without a Phoenix Gem."

The Manticore considered his words for a moment before shaking her head.

"No," she said, "my days of sending people on dangerous quests are over."

"What? Why?" asked Barley.

"Uh, 'cause they're dangerous!"

The hostess approached and told the Manticore that the karaoke machine was broken. They turned to see a group of angry bridesmaids and an irritated cyclops in a veil standing on a small stage.

The Manticore groaned in frustration and turned to the boys. "I'm sorry, but you're not getting this map." She rushed away to deal with the karaoke disaster.

The boys raced after her and watched as she stepped in and said sweetly, "Don't worry, ladies. Your adventure will continue momentarily!"

Ian approached the Manticore, determined to get the map. "Um, Miss Mighty Manticore, ma'am—"

"What are you doing?" Barley said through gritted teeth.

"Kid, this is not a good time," said the Manticore. The deafening screech of feedback from the microphone pierced the dining room chatter.

"I'm giving this place a one-star review!" shouted one of the bridesmaids.

"It's just, I never met my dad, and—" said Ian, still trying to reason with the Manticore.

"Look, I'm sorry about that, but if you get hurt on one of my quests, guess who gets sued and loses her tavern? I can't take that kind of risk! Now if you'll just excuse me, I have important things to do!" She tapped on the microphone. "Testing, testing."

"Please—we need that map!" insisted Ian.

"No, I am not giving you the map!" said the Manticore. "That's it! I'm done talking!" As customers started noticing the commotion, the Manticore tried to hide her anger by forcing a smile.

Ian stood up straight. "Well . . . well, I'm not!"

"Whoa!" said Barley, shocked by his brother's boldness.

The Manticore looked up, also surprised. Ian pointed to a portrait hanging on the wall. The Manticore looked fierce and heroic, wielding a giant sword.

"You say you can't *risk* losing this place?" said Ian.

"Look at that Manticore. She looks like she *lived* to take risks!"

She glanced at the painting and started gesturing wildly. "That Manticore didn't have investors to look out for. She didn't have payroll to cover! She could just fly out the door whenever she wanted and slay a magma beast."

One of the angry bridesmaids walked up to the Manticore with her hands on her hips. "Are you gonna fix the machine or not?"

"Yeah, in a minute!" shouted the Manticore. She turned back to Ian. "Okay, maybe this place isn't as adventurous as it used to be. So it isn't exactly filled with a motley horde willing to risk life and limb for the mere taste of excitement. . . ." She looked around, taking in the family-friendly scene. "But so what? Whoever said you have to take risks in life to have an adventure?"

Ian pointed behind the Manticore. "Apparently, you did."

The Manticore looked at the plaque above her portrait. It read YOU HAVE TO TAKE RISKS IN LIFE TO HAVE AN ADVENTURE. —THE MANTICORE

She was speechless.

A server dressed as a rogue approached, holding up a platter of fried food.

"Corey, table thirty-two said their mozzarella sticks are cold."

The Manticore breathed fire on the platter, scorching the food. Terrified, the server scuttled away.

"What have I done?" said the Manticore.

"Well, it's not too late," said Ian. "I mean, you could just give us the map—"

"This place used to be dangerous—" she continued, still lost in her realization.

The cuddly mascot stood behind the Manticore, dramatically imitating her. "Dangerous!"

"And wild," said the Manticore.

"Wild!" repeated the mascot.

"I used to be dangerous and wild!" said the Manticore.

"Dangerous and wild!" said the mascot.

Suddenly enraged, the Manticore tackled the mascot and ripped off its giant plush head! She held it up and growled, "I'm living a lie—WHAT HAVE I BECOME?" She ignited the mascot head with her fire breath!

"Oh, no . . . ," said Barley.

The Manticore threw the smoldering head and it landed on a table between two customers. "Everybody out! This tavern is closed for remodeling!"

With a deep breath, she spread her mighty wings. Then she let out a deafening roar!

8

Balloons popped and customers ran in terror, fleeing as the fire spread. "Sorry, the karaoke machine is broken!" the Manticore screeched, hurling it against the wall. Snarling, she picked up a smiling life-size cardboard cutout of herself and threw it into the flames. She dropped the map, and when Ian tried to get to it, it disappeared in a puff of ashes.

A heavy beam fell with a crash, just missing Ian and Barley. As the building began to crumble, they rushed toward the exit. In the chaos, Dad was thrown to the floor and another beam above him started to fall!

Without thinking, Ian lifted the staff and shouted, *"ALOFT ELEVAR!"* A blast of light magically held the beam in midair, inches from Dad! Ian strained to hold on to the spell as Barley rushed in and grabbed their dad, pulling him to safety.

Ian released the spell and the beam crashed to the floor. They hurried out of the burning tavern with Barley carrying Dad over his shoulder.

Safe inside the van, Barley pulled away from the building and headed down the road. He let out a relieved laugh. "That was unbelievable. You were just like . . ." He made some magical sound effects. "And the beam was just floatin' there! My brother is a wizard!"

Ian gave a small smile. "I can't believe that worked."

"Oh, you're gonna nail Dad's spell now," said Barley.

"Except we don't have a map."

"But we've got this! BEHOLD!" Barley revealed a kids' menu he had snatched on the way out. "Look, on a quest, you have to use what you've got. And this is what we've got." Barley pointed to a crayon signature: KAYLA. "Best part is, little Kayla already solved the puzzle."

Ian took the menu and studied the puzzle. "Well, according to Kayla, we just have to look for Raven's Point." He reached into the glove box and pulled out a modern map, placing it on the dash. He pointed to a mountain on the map. "Raven's Point!" He was suddenly taking the whole thing seriously.

"Yes! The gem must be in the mountain. We can be there by tomorrow morning," said Barley. "That still gives us plenty of time with Dad."

Ian looked at their dad. Then he put his finger on the tavern and traced a route to Raven's Point. "Well, it looks like the expressway should take us right there."

Barley shook his head. "Eh, expressway is a little too obvious. On a quest, the clear path is never the right one—"

Ian scrunched up his face in confusion. "What?"

Barley explained that during his Quests of Yore campaigns, he always followed his gut. "And it's telling me we take an ancient trail called the Path of Peril." He used his teeth to pull the cap off a pen and drew a line along a faint gray road on the map.

"But the expressway is faster," said Ian.

"Maybe not in the long run," said Barley.

"I know you want this to be like one of your adventure games, but all that matters is that we get to spend as much time as possible with Dad."

Stopped at a traffic light, Barley thought about

Ian's words as Dad moved to the front of the van. Barley patted his dad's foot.

"So we should just take the expressway," said Ian. "Right?"

"Yeah, you're right," said Barley. When the light turned green, he steered the van to the on-ramp that led to the expressway.

✦ ☽ ✦

Meanwhile, Laurel followed her GPS to the Manticore's Tavern as she talked to Colt on the phone. He had called to see whether she had found the boys.

"No, not yet," said Laurel. "I'm a little worried because we had a weird family issue come up, and well, this just isn't like Ian to run off. Barley, yes, but not Ian."

"You know, it's late. You shouldn't have to be out looking for them," said Colt.

"I know, it's silly. I'm sure they're both probably on fire—" Laurel said as she rounded the corner and saw the Manticore's Tavern in flames.

"Fire?" said Colt.

"FIRE! The place is on fire!" shouted Laurel. "My boys—I gotta go!" She quickly hung up.

Bright lights flashed as firefighters battled the

roaring flames. Laurel threw her car into park and leapt out, desperately searching for Barley and Ian. When she heard a voice nearby mention two teenage elves, she followed it to find the Manticore, wrapped in a silver thermal blanket and speaking to a police officer.

"Those are my sons! Where did they go?" Laurel asked urgently.

"They went on a quest to find a Phoenix Gem," said the Manticore. "But don't worry, don't worry. I told them about the map, and about the gem, and about the curse." She gasped. "I forgot to tell them about the curse!"

"The what?" asked Laurel.

"Hoo, boy . . . ," said the police officer, leaning toward Laurel. "Listen, this one's gone a little—" The officer let out a two-note whistle.

"Your boys are in grave danger!" said the Manticore. "But I can help—"

The officer stopped her. "Whoa, you're not going anywhere. We got questions for you," he said, guiding her toward his police car.

"I know where your boys are going!" exclaimed the Manticore. "We can still save them!"

Laurel looked around, desperate, trying to figure out what to do. A first-aid kit in an open ambulance nearby gave her an idea. Seconds later, she approached the Manticore and the police officer.

"Last name 'Manticore.' First name 'The'," said the Manticore.

"Hold on!" Laurel interrupted. She turned to the police officer. "You're right, she has gone—" Laurel let out the same two-note whistle the officer had. "It's no wonder, with a wound like that." She pointed to a small scrape on the Manticore's leg.

"That's just a scratch," said the officer.

Laurel pulled out the Quests of Yore card about the Manticore and waved it around like it was an official document. "Oh, I'm sorry—are you an expert on minotaurs?"

"Manticores," the Manticore corrected her.

"Manticores?" repeated Laurel.

"Well, no," said the officer.

"Well, then you wouldn't know that when their blood is exposed to air, it makes them go bonkers," said Laurel.

"I don't think that's true," said the Manticore.

Laurel pointed at her. "See! She's already losing her

grip on reality." Fully embracing her improvised role, Laurel stepped up to the officer. "So why don't you let me save her life before it costs you yours?"

The officer reluctantly agreed.

"Thank you!" said Laurel. "Could we have a little privacy here, please?"

He stepped behind the police car but listened as Laurel said, "Just lie back. That's good."

"Just don't take too long back there, okay?" said the officer. "Hey, you hear me?" He turned and looked at the Manticore's silhouette. "I said don't take too long back there, because I gotta get her to the——" As he walked around the side of the car, he saw the source of the shadow: the semi-melted head of the plush mascot! Laurel and the Manticore were gone!

The back of Laurel's car gave off sparks as it dragged against the asphalt, carrying the weight of the Manticore in the backseat.

"All right, how do we help my boys?" asked Laurel. She turned the steering wheel hard to race onto the expressway, slamming the Manticore against the door.

"Ooooooh, I'm gonna like you," said the Manticore, smiling over at Laurel.

9

As Barley drove, Ian sat next to Dad in the back of the van, looking down at the list he had made. He knew time was ticking away, and as he thought about it, a heavy realization washed over him. "Barley, we're not going to be able to get Dad back in time to see Mom."

Silence fell. Ian was right and there was nothing they could do to change it.

"Well, Dad . . . at least you won't have to meet the new guy," said Barley, finding the bright side. Then he put his finger up to his face for a pretend mustache and did his best Colt impression. *"So you, uh, workin' hard, or hardly workin'?"* He let out a loud horsey chuckle.

Ian laughed. *"Barley, Barley, Barley. Every time there's trouble, I gotta deal with you."* He cracked a proud smile at his performance.

"Is that your Colt?" said Barley in disbelief.

"Yeah?" said Ian, laughing.

"You're gonna wanna work on that."

Suddenly, the van began to sputter. Barley pulled off the expressway. "No, no, no, NO! Come on, old girl!" The engine wheezed one last time and the tires rolled a few more inches before the van came to a complete stop on the side of the road.

"I thought you said you fixed the van," said Ian with a groan.

"Relax, Guinevere's fine. Her stomach is just a little empty."

Ian glanced over at the gas gauge to see the needle firmly pointing to FULL. "But it says we have a full tank."

Barley looked at Ian like he was crazy. "Oh, that doesn't work." He climbed out, walked to the back of the van, and pulled out a gas can.

Ian watched as Barley shook the can. A tiny splash of gasoline sloshed around the bottom. "Only a few drops left. Maybe there's a gas station. . . ." Barley climbed on top of the van and looked around, but there was nothing in sight.

Ian groaned. Then he saw the staff. "Is there a magic way to get gas?"

Barley gasped. "Oooh! I like your thinking, young mage." He stumbled and fell to the ground. He popped back up holding out the guidebook, which showed an illustration of a wizard growing an apple to five times its size. "Growth Spell! We grow the can, and then the gas inside will grow with it."

"Uhh . . . that's kind of a weird idea . . . ," said Ian.

"I know! I like it, too!"

Ian muttered to himself as he held the staff. "Okay, loosen up, Heart's Fire. Here we go."

"Whoa, it's not that simple," said Barley, swaggering over to Ian. He turned to Dad and added, "This one learns a little magic and thinks he's Shamblefoot the Wondrous, am I right, Dad?"

Barley didn't notice as Ian shot him an annoyed glance.

"A Growth Spell is a bit more advanced," Barley explained. "Not only do you have to speak from your Heart's Fire, but now you also have to follow a magic decree."

"A magic what?"

Barley held up the open book. "It's a special rule that keeps the spell working right. This one states, 'To magnify an object, you have to magnify your attention upon it.' While you cast the spell, you can't let anything distract you." He placed the nearly empty gas can on the ground.

Ian stepped up and pointed the staff. "Okay. . . ." He took a deep breath. "Ow!"

"What?"

"Splinter!" said Ian, shaking his finger. "Can we sand this thing down?"

"No!" said Barley, incredulous. "It's an ancient staff with magic in every glorious fiber. You can't 'sand it down.'"

"All right, all right. Here we go," said Ian. "Focus. . . ." He held out the staff.

"Uh . . . ," Barley interrupted.

Ian frowned. "Something wrong?"

"Sorry, it's just, your stance is, uh . . ." Barley couldn't help intervening. He stood behind Ian and wrapped his arms around him like was showing him how to hold a golf club. He stood uncomfortably close as he maneuvered Ian's body, twisting it into an awkward pose. "Chin up, elbows out, feet apart, back slightly arched . . . Okay, how's that feel?"

"Great," said Ian, straining to hold the position.

"Oh! One more thing."

Ian took a deep frustrated breath, his patience wearing thin. Barley touched his elbow, raising it another inch. Then he stepped back for a moment before adjusting it a tad more. Ian shot him a look and Barley moved away.

Finally, Ian read the spell aloud. *"Magnora Gantuan!"* The staff lit up and sparks flew. He winced but did his best to stay focused. The can began to throb!

"Don't let the magic spook you," whispered Barley.

"Okay," said Ian, wishing his brother would stop talking.

"Elbows!" called Barley.

"What?"

"Elbows up!"

Ian lifted his elbows as high as possible.

"No, no, no, too high. That's too high," said Barley.

"I'm trying to focus here!" exclaimed Ian.

"Yeah, yeah, yeah, focus! Focus on the can!"

Ian tried with all his might to focus as the spell continued to throw sparks at him, and then . . . the can began to grow!

Excited, Barley whispered encouragement. "Focuuuuuuuuus. . . . Focuuuuuuuuusssssss. . . ."

"Barley!" shouted Ian, frustrated. "Ah, forget it!" Ian lost his concentration and the spell sputtered out, returning the gas can to its original size. He sighed.

"It worked! The can is huge!" said Barley in a squeaky voice.

Ian looked down to see . . . that Barley was tiny! His brother was about the size of a small water bottle!

"And the van is huge!" continued Barley. He looked up at Ian. "And you're—" Then it suddenly dawned on him. "Oh, no. . . ."

"What happened?" asked Ian.

"Looks like you shrunk me."

10

Tiny Barley walked over to the Quests of Yore book and gestured to the picture on the page he'd left it open to. "If you mess up a spell, there are consequences."

"I only messed up because you wouldn't stop bothering me!" said Ian.

"I was trying to help you!"

"Well, don't try to help me!"

"Oh, okay. Fine, I won't!"

As they argued, Dad tapped Ian's foot, then searched for Barley. He tapped Barley's head.

"Whooaaa, Dad. It's me!" said Barley. He returned the taps on Dad's foot. Dad's feet moved wildly as he realized Barley's size.

Ian tried to calm him down. "Whoa, Dad. It's okay, don't worry. I'm going to fix this!" He grabbed Dad's leash, picked up the empty gas can, and headed off in search of a gas station.

Barley insisted on going along but refused to let Ian carry him. He had to run to keep up, and it wasn't long before he was out of breath. "I just need a little break. My baby legs can't go that fast."

Ian walked back and picked up Barley by the back of his shirt. Barley kicked his feet, struggling, then suddenly stopped when he saw gas station lights up ahead. He pointed them out to Ian.

"Oh, wait, I forgot," said Barley, trying to turn away. "You don't need my help." He crossed his arms in defiance.

Ian dropped Barley into his front pocket and continued on.

"Hey! I don't need you to carry me!" exclaimed Barley. "I'm a grown man!"

When they reached the gas station, loud motorcycles pulled in, parking in front of the entrance. Ian squinted, trying to make out who—or what—was on the bikes.

Suddenly, a sprite in a leather jacket appeared, followed by other sprites. Several of them had been working together to drive each motorcycle! They were part of a motorcycle club called the Pixie Dusters. Ian stood back and watched as they sauntered through the door of the store.

An elf sipping a fruity frozen drink accidentally bumped into a sprite named Dewdrop.

"Hey! Did you just bump into me?" she demanded. The elf stammered as he tried to apologize. "Do it again and you'll see me in your nightmares!" The elf's drink slipped out of his hand and splattered on the ground as he hurried off.

Ian waited until all the sprites had gone into the store. Then he took a deep breath and slowly walked toward the entrance, leading Dad by the leash.

Inside, the sprites seemed to be everywhere. Some climbed the shelves, throwing items down to their friends, and others filled cups with soda or purchased candy.

"Uh, ten on pump two, please," whispered Ian, stepping up to the clerk.

Barley leaned out of Ian's pocket and reached for a bag of snacks on the counter, knocking the entire rack to the floor.

"What are you doing?" said Ian. His eyes darted around as he quickly cleaned up the mess. He wanted to get out before the sprites noticed them.

"I'm getting us food," explained Barley.

"All right, I got it. And a couple of these, thank you," Ian said to the clerk, placing a couple of the bags on the counter.

Barley tugged at Ian's shirt and told him he had to go to the bathroom.

"Can it wait?" asked Ian, irritated.

"It's your pocket," said Barley.

Ian sighed and got the bathroom key from the clerk. It dangled from an old license plate and was so heavy for tiny Barley that he had to carry it over his head. When he moved toward the bathroom, Dad searched with his foot and just missed stepping on him!

As Ian paid the cashier, Dad continued to search and accidentally tapped one of the sprites on the head.

"Hey! Watch it!" said the sprite.

Dewdrop hopped onto a shelf and grabbed Dad by the shirt collar. "You got a problem, Shades?" she said, staring into his sunglasses. Unable to respond, Dad appeared to simply stare back. "Answer me when I'm talking to you!"

Ian was terrified to see Dewdrop leaning aggressively into Dad. "Sorry," he said. "I don't really know where his head is at right now." He quickly pulled Dad toward the exit.

✦ ⭒ ☾ ✦ ⭒

Meanwhile, Laurel continued down the road with the right side of her car dragging from the weight of the Manticore, who was crammed into the passenger seat.

"You know, I would fly us to help your boys, but . . . the old wings aren't what they used to be," said the Manticore.

"Oh, that's fine," said Laurel. "So, about this curse—"

The Manticore wiggled her wings. "It's my own fault. I should be doing my wing exercises every morning, but you know how that goes. . . ."

"Please, the curse," said Laurel, frustrated. "What does it do?"

"Right! Sorry. It's a Guardian Curse. If your boys take the gem, the curse will rise up"—the Manticore lifted her sleeve to reveal an arm full of tattoos, and she pointed to an image of a red mist—"and assume the form of a mighty beast." Another tattoo illustrated the mist pressing rocks and trees together to form a ferocious beast. "It will battle your sons to the . . ." She caught herself and looked up at Laurel. "Well . . . how do your boys do in a crisis?"

"Not great!" said Laurel, worried. "One of them is afraid of everything, and the other isn't afraid of anything."

"Yeah, that skinny kid of yours is pretty fearless," said the Manticore.

"No, no. You mean the big one. Barley."

"No, the little guy. Woo, he really let me have it."

Laurel was confused but shook it off. "What? No, look . . . you said you could help them. Right?"

The Manticore pointed to a tattoo showing a dark circle in the heart of one of the beasts. "Every curse has a core, the center of its power," she said. "And only one weapon forged of the rarest metals can destroy it: my enchanted sword." She showed Laurel another tattoo of a glowing sword. The words on it read THE CURSE CRUSHER.

"Okay, but you don't seem to have that on you," said Laurel.

The Manticore looked at Laurel with her eyes full

of regret. "I sold it. Got in a little tax trouble a few years back. But don't worry—I know just where to find it."

Laurel nodded, determined. "I am on my way, boys," she said aloud. "Just try to stay out of trouble."

Ian finished pumping gas into the can and nervously looked around, eager for Barley to return from the bathroom. He suddenly heard a small angry voice in the distance.

"Who you calling whimsical?"

Ian turned to see Barley standing between two sprites.

"You got a lotta nerve," said Dewdrop.

"I'm just saying sprites used to fly around spreading delight," said Barley. "That's a *good* thing."

"Sprites can't fly!"

"Well, your wings don't work 'cause you stopped using them."

"You calling me lazy?" said Dewdrop. She sucked down what was left of a Sparkle Stick and hurled it to the ground.

"No, no. Not you. Your ancestors."

"What did you say about my ancestors?" Dewdrop said, puffing out her chest.

"I didn't mean lazy," said Barley. "I—"

Ian reached down and plucked Barley from the scene. "I'm sorry!" he said, looking down at the sprites. "Very sorry! He's sorry, too. You don't need to fly. Who needs to fly? I mean, you've got those great bikes!"

"What are you doing?" said Barley. "I was just discussing history!"

"Barley, I'm trying to take care of you and Dad, and you are not making it any easier!" said Ian, struggling with the leash. "Dad, come on!"

Dad had wandered to the other side of the line of parked motorcycles. As Ian tugged on the leash, Dad crashed into one of the bikes. It fell against the next bike, and one by one, they fell like dominoes, blocking the gas station door! Ian gasped.

The rest of the motorcycle club, now locked inside, furiously slammed into the glass door, eager to get out and attack.

"HEY! YOU'RE DEAD!" Dewdrop screamed.

With Barley in his pocket and Dad on the leash, Ian raced away as fast as he could. "We're dead! We're dead! We're dead!" he chanted as he picked up speed.

When he reached the van, he frantically filled the tank with gasoline.

"Relax. They won't be able to lift those bikes—" said Barley. The sudden roar of motorcycle engines sounded and Barley's face fell. "Oh, they are strong. . . ."

"We're gonna die, we're gonna die!" repeated Ian. They tried to open the door, but the van was locked. "What? Where are the keys?"

Barley looked through the window to see the keys dangling from the ignition. Motorcycle headlights appeared in the distance!

"I got this!" said Barley. He slid his body through the cracked window and managed to lift the lock.

Ian threw the gas can into the van, put Dad in, and slammed the door. He climbed in the passenger side. "Okay, Go! Go! Go!" Then he looked over at Barley, tiny and useless in the driver's seat, and realized . . . he had to drive. "No. No way. . . ."

"You're gonna have to!" said Barley.

Ian moved Barley and slid over into the driver's seat. With his whole body tense, Ian methodically adjusted the seat and mirrors. He could see the motorcycles coming around the corner in the rearview mirror! He turned the key, but nothing happened.

"Don't turn it all the way," explained Barley. "There's a sweet spot . . . not in the middle, but not quite at the end!"

Ian wiggled and jiggled the stubborn key. "Comeoncomeoncomeon!" he said, straining. "Come. On. Guinevere!"

11

As if responding to Ian's begging, the van sputtered to life, jostling him around. Driving Guinevere was like riding a bucking bull!

"Put it in O for 'Onward!'" urged Barley.

Ian wrapped his hand around the screwdriver jutting out from behind the steering wheel and pulled it down to the handwritten O. He slammed his foot on the gas, and the van lurched forward just as a sprite broke the driver's-side window using a spiked flail! Ian screamed and ducked as shards of glass rained into the van.

"DRIVE!" shouted Barley.

Ian turned the wheel hard, and as the sprites sped forward, he cut them off! Their bikes screeched as they swerved to avoid a collision.

Ian managed to get farther ahead of them and soon approached the expressway on-ramp. The road roared with the sound of speeding cars. Ian cautiously pressed his foot on the gas pedal. After a small car passed, a huge freight truck barreled up.

"Speed up!" urged Barley. The ramp was about to end!

Ian held the wheel tight, sweat pouring from his brow. "I can't do this!"

"Yes, you can!"

"I'm not ready!"

"You'll never be ready! MERGE!"

Ian screamed as he stomped on the gas, sending Dad flying to the back of the van. Ian cut off the huge truck, barely missing its front bumper just as the ramp ended!

Once they were safe within the speeding traffic, Barley laughed, relieved. "Nice job!"

Ian glanced in the rearview mirror—the motorcycles had caught up and were right behind them! One of the sprites swung a flail above his head before releasing it, smacking the side of the van.

Barley leapt up to the window. "Hey, don't hit Gwinny!" he yelled to the sprites.

Ian swerved as he grabbed Barley and put him back in his seat. He gasped when he found himself behind a slow-moving car. Seeing their moment, the Pixie Dusters roared up behind them again. Barley jumped onto Ian's shoulder, directing him. "Get around 'em!"

Ian started to turn into the left lane. "They're not letting me in!"

"SIGNAL!" ordered Barley.

"You don't have a signal-er!" said Ian, frantically searching for it.

"Stick your arm straight out the window to signal left!" instructed Barley.

Ian held his arm out the window, and a sprite wrapped a chain around it, forcing him to drive with one hand! With great effort, he turned the wheel to move into the left lane. Barley carefully climbed out onto Ian's arm.

"Get back here!" cried Ian.

"Just keep driving!" said Barley, trying to untangle the chain.

The sprites cheered as they revved their motorcycles. Barley managed to get the chain off and it recoiled, knocking a bunch of the shocked sprites off their bike!

Ian looked ahead and saw the expressway splitting into north and south.

Barley crawled back onto Ian's shoulder. "The mountains are north. You need to get all the way over!"

Dewdrop spotted Dad's top half flapping out the window in the wind. The stuffed arm looked like he was shaking a fist. She narrowed her eyes. "Oh, it is *on*, Shades!" Dewdrop and her crew gunned their motorcycle. "Get 'em!"

The bike pulled up alongside Ian's open window, and a crew of sprites leapt in! They screamed as they began attacking Ian and Dad, punching, pinching, and pulling at them. One of the sprites tackled Barley, and they hit the dashboard next to a warrior bobblehead. Barley pulled the sword from the bobblehead and brandished it at his foe.

Soon Ian had sprites all over his face. Unable to see, he steered the van right into the guardrail! Barley and the sprite he was battling were thrown from the dashboard onto the passenger seat.

"Ian! Stay focused!" said Barley.

"I can't!" shouted Ian.

"You HAVE to focus or we're all dead!" said Barley. "Just stay cool!"

Barley's words gave Ian an idea. He frantically felt around the control panel and flicked on the air-conditioning. Powerful air blasted out of the vents, blowing all the sprites right out the windows!

Barley saved himself by clinging to the seat belt. "Way to go, Guinevere!" he cheered as his body flapped in the breeze. But he suddenly lost his grip and flew out the window, too! Without missing a beat, Ian stuck his hand out and caught him. Then he switched off the AC.

They were very close to the exit.

"We're not gonna make it!" cried Barley.

Refusing to back down, Ian smoothly crossed several lanes of traffic, just making it onto the ramp to head north! The van hurtled toward a wall and a tire hit the edge. Guinevere was airborne for a brief moment before crashing back down to the ground!

The sprites were right on Ian's tail and couldn't steer away from the wall in time. They screamed as they crashed into it! Ian watched in the rearview mirror as they were thrown off their bikes into the air. Suddenly, their wings began to flap—they were flying!

Tiny Barley was perched on Ian's shoulder, celebrating their victory, as Ian continued to drive. Ian leaned toward the back and asked Dad if he was okay.

Barley smiled. "He's fine, thanks to the skillful driving of Sir Ian Lightfoot! High-five!" He raised his tiny hand to slap Ian's, but it bulged to full size just then and slammed into the roof of the van.

"I think the spell is wearing off," said Barley. Then his torso expanded to full size on Ian's shoulder, causing Ian to swerve. Cars honked as the van veered all over the road.

"Get off my face!" Ian shouted.

Barley's right leg expanded. His foot reached the floor and slammed the gas pedal! The van flew forward and slid into the side of the road, sputtering across the dirt. The back door popped open. Ian didn't realize he'd zipped past a hidden police car. The officer instantly fired up the lights and sirens and peeled after the van.

12

Barley, now back to his regular size, climbed into the passenger seat while Ian gained control of the vehicle.

"Oh, Chantar's Talon! Cops!" said Ian, staring at the flashing lights behind him.

"Pull over!" shouted Barley.

"I don't have a license," said Ian.

Barley reached into his pocket and screamed as he pulled out a small bit of folded leather. "My wallet's still tiny!"

Ian slowed the van and moved to the shoulder. Officer Specter, a cyclops, and Officer Gore, a satyr, emerged from the police car.

"Step out of the vehicle," ordered Officer Specter through a speaker.

As the boys looked at each other, trying to figure out

what to do, Dad wandered around the back and toward the open door! The officers exchanged a look as they watched Dad stumble out of the van onto the road.

"You have a long night there, buddy?" asked Officer Gore.

The boys crouched next to the passenger door to stay hidden as they watched the officers approach Dad.

"Sir, I'm gonna ask you to walk this straight line," said Officer Specter.

"They're gonna take Dad!" whispered Ian, horrified.

Barley thought for a moment. "Oh! I got it! The Disguise Spell! You can disguise yourself to be anyone you want." He used his finger to draw the spell on the side of the dirty van.

"What if I mess up again?" whispered Ian.

"According to the spell, 'Disguising yourself is a lie, so you must tell the truth to get by.' As long as you don't tell a lie, the spell will be fine."

"Okay . . . who are we gonna be?" asked Ian. Barley smiled as an idea crossed his mind.

Moments later, there was a dim flash behind the van and a faint magical crackling, followed by a *CLOMP, CLOMP, CLOMP, CLOMP.* The cops turned to see . . . Officer Colt Bronco!

The spell had worked! The boys were magically masked by a ghostlike shell of Colt. Ian "wore" the front part of the illusion while Barley had the back. As Ian impersonated Colt, the officers saw and heard Colt!

Colt appeared to be a little nervous. "What seems to be the problem here, fellow . . . police folk?"

The officers were surprised to see him. "Were you . . . in that van?" Officer Specter asked.

"Affirmative!" he said, still sounding a little unsure. "And we will, I mean, *I* will take full responsibility for that fella right there, so you can just release him over to me."

Barley whispered up to Ian, "Hey, I wanted to be the front."

"No way, I'll do the talking," whispered Ian.

"Bronco, I thought you were working on the other side of town," said Officer Gore.

"I, uh, changed my mind," Ian answered. Just then, Colt's right horse ear vanished! Ian realized he had slipped up. His lie had caused a small part of the disguise to disappear! He quickly turned to hide the missing ear from the officers.

"Something wrong?" asked Officer Specter, suspicious.

"Just a little . . . neck . . . cramp!" he lied. Colt's

left hand disappeared! Ian quickly bent his arm to hide the missing body part, contorting himself.

"The spell is disappearing!" Ian whispered.

"You have to stop lying. Answer every question with a question!" Barley warned.

"What exactly are you doing out here?" asked Officer Specter.

"Uh . . . ," Ian stammered as he carefully thought about how he should respond. "What am I doing out here?" He gave a nervous chuckle. "What are any of us doing out here?"

"Whoa . . . ," said Officer Gore, nodding in deep thought. "I never thought about it like that."

"Nice!" whispered Barley, impressed.

"With all due respect, you didn't answer my question," said Officer Specter.

"Well, we were just exercising some driver's education drills for . . . Ian," explained Colt.

"Who is Ian?" asked Officer Specter.

Officer Gore pointed back to Dad. "Oh, is that Laurel's kid?"

"Ian is Laurel's kid," answered Colt.

"Your stepson was swerving all over the road," said Officer Specter.

"Yeah, well . . . that guy's not all there today," he said, pointing to Dad. They looked back to see Dad slumped over the hood of the police car.

"Yeah, he does seem a little off," Officer Specter said.

"Uh, actually, if I'm being completely honest . . . I'm not super great in this kinda situation . . . and I'm starting to freak out a little bit. I'm all sweaty and weird, and I don't know what to say and I just feel like I can't do anything right, and I'm a total weirdo—"

Specter approached, suddenly calm. "Whoa, whoa, hold on, okay, hold on, hold on. I think I know what's going on here."

"You do?"

"Yeah, it's not easy being a new parent. My girlfriend's daughter's got me pulling my hair out."

The officers chuckled and waved them on.

"Keep workin' hard . . . or hardly workin'," said Colt. Then he let out a hearty horsey laugh as the boys worked together to maneuver Dad back into the van.

"Now, that was a good Colt!" whispered Barley.

"I don't envy you, Bronco. That Lightfoot kid is a handful," said Officer Gore.

"I'm gonna have to disagree with you there," said

Colt. "I think Ian's a pretty stand-up citizen."

"Not him, the older one," said Officer Gore.

The statement stopped Ian in his tracks.

"I mean, the guy's a screwup. You can't say you don't agree?" Officer Gore continued.

"Um, I don't," said Ian. Colt's right leg vanished! Ian quickly bent his leg behind the other to hide it. Barley couldn't believe what he was seeing.

"I mean, um, uh, okay, well, um, I have to get going. Gotta get Ian home." Colt's other ear vanished and he quickly began to shuffle back to the van. "Ah, I mean, I'm late for work." As he rambled on, nervously telling lie after lie, the Colt illusion continued to fall away. The brothers just managed to slip into the van before the spell vanished completely.

"Oh man, Bronco is losing it," said Officer Gore while Specter suspiciously watched the van drive away. "That's why I never got married. Yup, Old Gore can't be tied down."

Specter flipped on her flashlight and examined Colt's hoofprints in the dirt. Following them, she saw that they transformed into shoe prints! She picked up her radio. "This is Specter. Can you put me through to Officer Colt Bronco?"

13

A heavy silence hung in the van. Barley stared at the road ahead as he drove.

Finally, Ian spoke. "Barley . . . I don't know what happened back there, but I don't think you're a screwup." Barley didn't say a word. "Maybe the magic just got it wrong . . . you know?"

Barley snapped on the stereo and turned the volume way up, playing some heavy metal music to tune his brother out.

"I DON'T KNOW WHAT HAPPENED!" Ian shouted over the blaring electric guitar.

Barley raised the volume even higher. Ian continued to yell, and suddenly, Barley whipped off the expressway and pulled into a deserted rest stop.

He quickly got out of the van, leaving the loud music on, and angrily ripped open a bag of cheese puffs.

"Where are you going?" called Ian, following him. "Barley, come on. This is all just—"

Barley stopped and turned to face Ian. "I'm not a screwup!" he shouted, finally letting out some of his anger.

"I didn't say you were."

"The magic said it for you!"

"Well, *the magic* got it wrong!"

"Magic doesn't get it wrong! The cop asked a question, you answered, and the magic revealed the truth. RIGHT?"

"I don't know how any of this stuff works!" said Ian. "All I know is that everything we've done tonight has gone wrong!"

"It's gone wrong because you won't listen to me!" said Barley.

Ian was stunned. "Are you kidding? Because everything we've done today has been your idea—"

"But you didn't do it *my* way! You didn't let me handle the Manticore. You freaked out when I talked to the sprites. Because you don't think I have good ideas."

"What! Of course I do!" insisted Ian.

"Great, then I think we should take the Path of Peril!"

Ian paused. "And I also think that would be good . . . normally—"

"See!" said Barley.

"But I told you, this isn't a game! All that matters today is Dad, and right now, he's sitting in that van, and he's confused—" Ian stopped talking as he noticed Barley looking over Ian's shoulder, distracted.

He turned to follow Barley's gaze and saw Dad standing in the back of the van, awkwardly bopping to the music.

"I think he can feel the vibrations of the music, and he's . . . dancing," said Barley, his anger fading.

Before long, Dad was really getting into it, jutting out his butt and pointing his toes.

"*Wow.* He is terrible," said Ian.

"Yeah. He's really, really bad," agreed Barley.

Dad flailed so wildly that his phony top half fell off. Suddenly, he shimmied his way over to the boys.

"Oh, no, here he comes," said Barley.

Dad hooked his leg around Barley and dragged him over to his makeshift dance floor.

"No, no, no. Thanks, Dad. Dad, thank you! I'm good! Stop!" said Barley, trying to resist. But Dad wouldn't give up, and finally Barley joined him, laughing as he danced along.

Ian watched for only a moment before Dad wiggled forward. Ian tried to avoid him, too, but Dad wouldn't have it. Before long, the three of them were enjoying Dad's awkward dance party together, shaking their troubles loose.

"Just imagine what the top half of this dance looks like," said Ian.

"I bet it goes something like this!" said Barley. He stepped behind Dad and danced wildly, filling out the missing body parts. The boys laughed and laughed.

When the music stopped, Dad sat down, seemingly exhausted.

"Oh, you danced your shoelaces loose, there, Pop," said Barley. He kneeled and tied his dad's shoe. Barley looked up at Ian. "You know, I want to see him, too."

"Yeah . . . I know."

Barley stood. "It's not fair for you to call me a screwup if you don't give me a chance to get something right. Just do one thing my way."

"You really think this Path of Peril is the best way to go to the mountain?"

Barley nodded.

Ian looked uncertain as he thought for a moment before saying, "Okay."

Barley grinned.

They hopped back into the van, and instead of getting back onto the expressway, they turned down a dusty, unpaved road. They didn't realize it, but the rough terrain shook Guinevere's rear bumper right off.

The world was once full of magic! Majestic unicorns soared through the sky, mermaids frolicked in the ocean waves, and wizards used sorcery to help everyone in need.

As time went by, technology replaced magic. Now everyone uses phones, cars, and planes to get by. Life may be easier, but it's much less adventurous than it used to be.

Barley Lightfoot is a big, bold, and boisterous elf. He yearns for the days of magic and quests. He imagines himself a hero of those forgotten times, and he craves ADVENTURE!

Ian Lightfoot is Barley's younger brother. He is shy and awkward. He isn't eager for adventure, but he does wish he were a bit more confident.

Ian and Barley's father passed away before Ian was born. Ian always listens to a tape recording of his dad's voice. He wishes more than anything that he'd known his dad.

Laurel, Ian and Barley's mom, has a surprise—a gift from Dad! He told Laurel to give it to the boys only after they had both turned sixteen.

The gift is a spell, a Phoenix Gem, and a wizard's staff. With these objects, they can bring Dad back to life for one day!

Barley tries first, but nothing happens. After Ian recites the spell, light bursts from the staff. Barley proclaims that his little brother has the gift of magic.

The family's pet dragon, Blazey, arrives to investigate the commotion.

The spell only brings back Dad's bottom half! Ian makes a disguise for him, and they set off on a quest. They need to find another Phoenix Gem to complete the spell.

Along the way, Barley's van, Guinevere, runs out of gas. Ian tries to use a Growth Spell to increase the amount they have, but . . .

. . . he accidentally shrinks Barley instead!

Ian and Barley encounter a motorcycle club of sprites called the Pixie Dusters. The leader, Dewdrop, gets angry at the boys.

The Pixie Dusters chase Guinevere! Even though he's scared of driving, Ian takes the wheel and escapes the sprites.

The boys arrive at the Path of Peril, where they find a bottomless pit. Ian will need to get them across using magic. Barley ties a rope around him in case he falls.

Ian creates an invisible bridge to cross the pit! But time is running out. . . . Will Ian and Barley be able to find another Phoenix Gem?

14

Laurel and the Manticore pulled up to an old, unremarkable pawnshop. Laurel didn't understand why they were there.

"If we don't leave here with the sword, your boys are doomed," said the Manticore.

The place was packed with things like old televisions, armor, books, and tarnished musical instruments. A grizzled, lanky goblin named Grecklin placed a large garlic press on the counter.

"There you are—one garlic crusher," she said.

"No, *Curse* Crusher. It's a large magical sword," said the Manticore, frustrated.

"Sword, sword, sword," said Grecklin, thinking. She looked through the junk behind the counter until finally, she held up a huge and glorious sword. "I mean, I got this thing," she added.

The Manticore gasped. "That's it!"

"How much?" asked Laurel.

"Oh," said Grecklin, looking at it, unimpressed. "Let's call it, uh . . . ten."

"Great!" said Laurel, digging through her wallet.

As she counted out the money, the Manticore gazed at the gleaming sword, bursting with emotion. "Forged of the rarest metals, the only sword of its kind in all the land. Hello, old friend. We shall never part again."

Laurel finished paying, and the Manticore reached for the sword, but Grecklin slammed her hand down on it.

"Oops," she said with an evil smile. "Turns out this sword is the only sword of its kind in all the land. So . . . let's call it ten . . . thousand."

"You can't do that!" shouted Laurel.

Grecklin shrugged. "Well, I just did."

"Well, you had better—" Laurel's phone rang and she stepped away to answer. It was Colt.

"Hey, I talked to some other officers, and they said the boys were last seen going north."

"Are they okay?" asked Laurel.

"They're fine, but the officers said . . . Well . . . honey, this night keeps getting stranger and stranger."

Laurel glanced up as the Manticore leaned toward Grecklin. "Do you know who I am?" the Manticore demanded.

"Some kind of winged bear-snake lady?" said Grecklin.

"Winged *lion-scorpion* lady!" the Manticore snarled.

Laurel focused back on her phone conversation. "It sure does." She walked over to Grecklin. "Listen, I need that sword. My sons have a once-in-a-lifetime chance to see their father. Now, my oldest son——"

Suddenly, the Manticore whipped her scorpion tail, striking Grecklin in the neck! Grecklin's eyes popped open and she collapsed!

Laurel shrieked. "HOLY— SON OF— YOU KILLED HER!"

"It's okay!" said the Manticore. "She's only temporarily paralyzed."

They peered over the counter to see Grecklin on the floor, motionless. Grecklin mumbled through stiff lips, "Hey! You can't do this."

"Well, I just did," said the Manticore, echoing Grecklin's rude line.

Laurel shouted, "Grab the sword!"

"Don't you touch that!" said Grecklin.

The Manticore took the Curse Crusher.

"Here you go," Laurel said politely as she placed some cash on the counter. "And a little something extra for your trouble."

As they exited the store, Laurel flipped the sign on the door to read CLOSED.

Running to the car, Laurel and the Manticore cheered. Colt was still on the other end of the phone.

"Hello?" he called. "Are you all right?! Laurel?"

Laurel picked up the phone. "Oh, Colt, I can't talk! The boys need me!" Then she hung up.

Colt sat in his car, frustrated and worried. "Wait! Dang those kids."

As he drove toward the expressway, something in the road caught his eye . . . a beat-up rear bumper. He pulled up next to it to investigate and saw the license plate: GWNIVER. Colt pressed his hoof on the gas and sped down the unpaved road.

Dad and Ian snoozed in the back of the van while Barley happily sang as he drove along.

"We're heading on our quest, our father we must retrieve, the Lightfoot Brothers can't be stopped . . . something, something that rhymes with retrieved!"

The van hit a bump, and Ian and Dad woke with a jolt. Barley chuckled. "Well, good morning to thee, dear Lightfoot men! Welcome to the Path of Peril!"

Ian blinked the sleep from his eyes and looked out the window. Open fields stretched as far as he could see. "It's not much of a path."

"Well, you know, they never really developed around here. So heads up. We could run into anything. . . ."

Barley began scanning the area, taking his eyes off the road ahead.

Suddenly, Ian saw a huge drop right in front of them! "WHOA! STOP!"

Barley slammed on the brakes with a scream. The boys stepped out of the van to see that they were at the edge of what appeared to be a bottomless chasm.

Ian held Dad's leash as he looked over the edge. "What is this?"

"Bottomless Pit," explained Barley. "Whatever falls in there falls forever."

He pointed out an ancient drawbridge, poised to stretch across the wide chasm. "We lower that bad boy and we are on our way to Raven's Point. Look around for a lever."

"Found it! But it's on the other side," said Ian, pointing across the massive pit. He handed Dad's leash to Barley and lifted the staff. "Okay, I got this. *Aloft Elevar!*" Magic shot out of the staff, but it disappeared halfway across the chasm.

"You can't cast a Levitation Spell on something that far away!" said Barley. "It only has like a fifteen-meter enchanting radius." He giggled. "Dad, can you believe this guy?"

Ian stared blankly, not appreciating the humor.

"What we need is a Trust Bridge," explained Barley. "It's a spell that creates a magical bridge you can walk on. Just say, *'Bridgrigar Invisia.'*"

Ian practiced saying the words a few times before moving to the edge of the chasm. He held out his staff and proclaimed, *"Bridgrigar Invisia."* The staff lit up . . . but there was no bridge. "It didn't work."

Barley pointed out that the staff was glowing. "No, the spell's still going. You won't know if your bridge worked until you step on it."

"Step on what?" asked Ian, confused.

"If you believe the bridge is there, then it's there," said Barley.

Ian looked at his brother like he was talking nonsense. "But it's not."

"Well, not with that attitude," said Barley.

Ian gestured to the empty air over the pit. "I'm not going to step out onto nothing!"

Moments later, Barley was tying a thick rope around Ian's waist. He anchored the other end to a nearby tree. Dad sat in the front seat of the van with the window down and his feet resting on the dash, as if he was watching them.

Barley gave the rope a tug, testing it out. He grabbed the middle of the rope and looked at Ian, who stood at the edge of the pit. The staff continued to glow.

"Now we've got a rope," said Barley. "But you're not even going to need it because—"

"I WANT THE ROPE!" shouted Ian.

"I'm just saying, you're not gonna need the rope because I know you can make that bridge."

Ian took a deep breath. Then he stepped over the edge . . . and fell! Barley yanked on the rope, stopping Ian a few feet down.

"I'm dying, I'm dying! I'm dead! I'm dead! My life is over!" screamed Ian.

"I've got you!" said Barley, holding on to the rope. He pulled Ian back up to solid ground and dusted him off. "Okay, you fell. But was that so bad?"

"YES!"

"Are you still alive?" Barley asked calmly.

"Yes," said Ian, considering that fact for a moment.

"Okay, so now you know the worst that can happen. So there's nothing to be scared of, right?"

Ian looked across the chasm to the other side. He took a deep breath, repositioned himself at the edge, and said, *"Bridgrigar Invisia!"* The staff pulsed with a magical glow. Ian glanced down into the pit, then back at Barley.

"Hey. You can do this," Barley said with certainty.

Ian closed his eyes and stepped off the edge. His foot stopped in midair—and planted itself on a glowing blue light that had just appeared!

"THERE YOU GO!" cheered Barley.

Ian stood for a moment holding his other leg up before slowly placing it down. But as he felt around, there was nothing there.

Barley tugged on the rope, pulling him back. Then he shouted, "Believe with every step!"

Ian probed again, hoping to find something solid. He closed his eyes, concentrated . . . and landed on another blue glow.

"Oh, yeah!" said Barley.

Ian took another step, and another.

"You've got me, right?" called Ian, suddenly feeling giddy.

"I still got you!" said Barley. "WOO-HOO! Ian Lightfoot is FEARLESS!"

Ian smiled. As if walking on air, he took one confident step after another, and soon he was standing in the middle of the chasm!

Ian didn't notice, but the knot in the rope around his waist began to loosen. Barley's eyes popped open wide at the sight.

"This is amazing!" cheered Ian, still unaware of the loosening knot. As he took a few more steps, the rope completely untied and fell into the pit!

"Yeah, but keep going! Don't look back! Just straight ahead!" said Barley, trying to hide his anxiety.

Ian howled with laughter, feeling incredible. "You've still got the rope, right?"

Barley looked down at the useless end of rope he still held in his hands. "YEAH! I GOT IT!"

"I AM NOT AFRAID!" announced Ian, marching forward. He felt like a different person, suddenly fearless and bold. "Oh, man, I could stay out here all day!" He playfully shifted his feet from side to side, landing on magical light every time.

"OKAY, BUT KEEP MOVING!" said Barley, trying very hard not to reveal how terrified he was. "WE'VE GOTTA SEE DAD, REMEMBER?"

Ian approached the other side. "HEY, DAD, THIS LAST STEP IS FOR YOU!" But when he looked over his shoulder toward Dad, he saw the rope hanging down into the pit. His confidence vanished, and so did the magic. Barley watched, horrified, as his brother plunged into nothingness.

15

But just in time, Ian managed to grab the edge of the pit's rocky rim. Using all his might, he pulled himself up to solid ground and leaned against the bridge's lever. The old drawbridge creaked as it slowly lowered and touched down on the other side.

Barley laughed, overjoyed. "He did it, Dad!" Ian tried to catch his breath as he watched Barley hop into the van and drive across the bridge.

As soon as he parked, Barley jumped out to hug Ian. "That was amazing!"

Ian stood still as stone. "How long was the rope gone?"

"Oh, just like the second half of it," said Barley nonchalantly.

"I needed that rope!"

"Oh, but did you?"

Ian's anxious expression melted away. A smile crept across his face as he considered what he had just accomplished.

Barley gasped and pointed to a sculpture of a raven that had been revealed when the bridge was lowered. He took out the wrinkled children's menu and showed Ian. "The clue on the menu said Raven's Point. . . ."

"Yeah. In the mountains."

"But maybe the puzzle didn't mean the mountain," said Barley. "Maybe it means 'Follow where the raven is pointing!'" He looked up and tracked the line of the raven's beak. Another raven statue stood in the distance! "That one could be pointing to another raven, all the way to the gem!"

Ian couldn't believe it. "I had us going the wrong way."

"Well, I told ya. My gut knows where to go." Barley looked down at his stomach and gave it a pat. "Don't ya, boy? Yes, you do!"

Ian couldn't help smiling at his brother, impressed.

"Come on, Dad!" called Barley. He led Dad to the

van and jingled his keys in the air. "Guinevere will get us to that raven in no time!"

Just then, a siren blared, drawing their attention back to the bridge. A police car sped across it, screeching to a halt in front of them. The door flew opened to reveal Colt. "You guys are in trouble, big-time!" he said, straining to get out of the car.

"No, no, no, Colt—we found a spell," explained Barley. "If we finish it before sunset, we'll get to see our father." Barley showed Dad's legs to Colt.

"Well, uh, your mom told me there was some kind of strange . . . family issue going on, and this is . . . definitely strange," Colt muttered, trying to figure out what he was looking at. Determined to stay focused, he shook his curiosity away. "But no, dang it. I'm not letting you upset your mother any more! Now, you get in the vehicle. I'm escorting you home."

"No, no way!" exclaimed Barley.

"I'm giving you to the count of three." Colt stomped his hoof, once, twice, and then . . .

"Okay. We'll go," said Ian, grabbing the keys from Barley.

"Ian—" said Barley, disappointed to see his brother surrendering so easily.

"He's a police officer," said Ian. He turned and headed toward the driver's side of the van. Colt watched and nodded to Ian gratefully.

They climbed in and Barley looked at Ian, surprised to see him getting behind the wheel. "What are you doing?"

"I don't know," said Ian. Then he stomped on the gas pedal and took off! Barley looked through the back window to see Colt standing there, completely stunned.

"HA-HA, YEAH!" cheered Barley. "Iandore Lightfoot, breaking the rules!"

"I can't believe I'm running from the cops!"

"You're not running from the cops. You're running from our mom's boyfriend."

Sirens blared and lights flashed. Ian looked in the rearview mirror to see several police cars behind Colt's!

"Okay, *now* you're running from the cops," said Barley.

Ian veered off the path, crashing into a fence. Wood debris flew everywhere! The police cars swerved to follow Guinevere. Ian spotted a raven statue in the distance, and the van fishtailed as he whipped around a tight corner to get closer to it. He sped up and turned down another narrow mountain pass that quickly became a dead end! He swung the van around, but the police cars were already starting down the road. There was no escape!

They climbed out of the van with Dad, and Ian felt a rush of regret. "Oh, what did I do? I shouldn't have driven away—"

"No, it was great!" said Barley. He pointed to some boulders hanging over the pass. "Block the road with those boulders!"

"What?! How?"

"Arcane Lightning."

"You said that's the hardest spell," said Ian nervously.

"You are ready."

Barley handed Ian the Quests of Yore book and pointed to the spell. " *'To make lightning strike with ease, one must follow all decrees.'* You have to do everything. Speak from your Heart's Fire, trust yourself, focus, all of it!"

Ian picked up the staff and pointed it at the boulders. *"Voltar Thundasir,"* he said, uncertain. *"Voltar Thundasir."*

A small lightning bolt shot from the staff and

pinged off the boulders. He tried again, but his magic wasn't strong enough to move the boulders even a little bit.

"I can't. I can't do it!" groaned Ian. The police cars were rapidly getting closer. "We're not gonna see you, Dad. And it's all my fault." Ian couldn't believe his chance of meeting his father was slipping away.

Barley thought for a moment before making a decision. With a pained expression, he popped a tape into the van's tape deck. Sad, heroic music blared from the speakers.

Ian asked Barley what he was doing, but he didn't answer. He was busy working. He aimed Guinevere like he was lining up a pool shot, then picked up a large rock and placed it on the gas pedal. He knocked the screwdriver gearshift down to O.

The brothers watched as Guinevere lurched forward. One of her turn-signal lights fell to the ground, but she continued, racing toward the boulders. Then the rocky terrain popped one of her tires, causing her to bounce along the ground as though in a gallop. With the music blaring triumphantly, the glove compartment flew open. Parking tickets fluttered out into the wind like celebratory doves. Ian watched in awe as Barley saluted his beloved Guinevere for the last time.

Just as the police cars approached, the van slammed into the target and flipped over. Piles of boulders rained down, surrounding Guinevere, completely blocking the road. It was impossible for the police cars to get through.

Barley bent and picked up Guinevere's turn-signal light. He gave it a loving rub before gently slipping it into his pocket.

"Barley . . . ," Ian began, unsure of what to say.

"She was just a beat-up old van," said Barley, burying his emotions. "Come on, we gotta go."

Barley walked off the road and started through the brush toward the raven statue. For a moment, Ian looked back at the boulders covering Guinevere, then at Barley walking ahead with Dad. He hurried to catch up with them.

16

The boys and Dad walked in silence until they reached the raven statue. Just as Barley had thought, its beak pointed to another raven in the distance. They continued walking from raven to raven until they finally reached one near a small river. Barley pulled some overgrowth aside to reveal its beak. Unlike the others, it pointed straight down, toward a disk buried in the ground. Barley began to pull at it.

Then Ian noticed something on the disk. "Wait," he said, wiping some dirt away. They could see the reflection of the raven's chest in the disk. Ian felt the statue with his fingers and pulled out a loose clover-shaped stone!

"You see that, Dad?" said Barley, impressed. "The apprentice has become the master." Barley took a closer look at the stone and saw that it was engraved with a few wavy lines and an X. He thought the wavy lines looked like water.

Ian looked around and pointed at a small river flowing into a tunnel. "So what's the X mean?"

"On a quest, an X only means one thing," said Barley, smiling. "We go to the end of the water, we'll find that Phoenix Gem."

They stepped down to the river and entered the dark tunnel. Ian used magic to light a torch, guiding the way. Then they were startled by a group of horrific-looking unicorns huddled in a corner! The boys screamed as the creatures hissed and fluttered away.

"Unicorns! Ugh!" said Ian with a shiver.

As they walked along the bank of the river, past ancient paintings on the tunnel walls, Barley snacked on cheese puffs while Ian held the torch. Ian tried to see the tunnel's end, but he couldn't.

"This water could go on for miles," said Ian. "We don't have that kind of time."

"If we had something to float on, we could cast a Velocity Spell on it and fly down the tunnel like a magic Jet Ski," said Barley.

Ian looked around but didn't see anything useful.

"Remember, on a quest, you have to use what you've got," said Barley. He looked down at a cheese puff in his hand and grinned.

Moments later, Ian recited the magic words *"Magnora Gantuan!"* Light flashed, and suddenly Ian, Barley, and Dad were floating on a giant cheese puff! Ian wielded the staff and commanded, *"Accelior!"*

The cheese-puff boat zoomed into the darkness.

"This is actually kind of cool!" said Ian. "So, what other spells do you know?"

"Ooh, brace yourself, young mage. I can show you all there is to know of magic!"

Meanwhile, Laurel and the Manticore continued making their way toward Ian and Barley. But without warning, a flying sprite hit the windshield! Laurel and the Manticore screamed. With the sprite blocking her view, Laurel drove the car off the road and into a ditch.

"I think I stung my leg," said the Manticore, kicking the door open.

They got out of the car, feeling a little dazed.

The sprite peeled herself off the windshield. "You almost killed me, lady!"

"Are you okay?" asked Laurel. "Where did you come from?"

Suddenly, more sprites swooped down, Dewdrop among them. "You were in our flight path!" she said.

The Manticore took in the sight of the car. The front was smashed, and smoke puffed out of the engine.

"Oh, no!" she said. "Our transport! How are we going to get to your sons now?"

Laurel looked around for a sign of hope and watched as the sprites rose into the air.

"Come on, Pixie Dusters. Let's take to the skies!" called Dewdrop, leading them in flight.

Watching the sprites fly off into the distance, Laurel got an idea. She turned to the Manticore. "How do you feel about exercising those wings?"

The Manticore fluttered her wings nervously.

The boys continued speeding through the tunnel on the cheese-puff boat. Ian stood holding the staff as Barley helped him learn a new spell.

"Boombastia!" shouted Ian, causing a small spark to ignite.

Ian didn't mind it when Barley adjusted his shoulder

a little, reminding him of the proper posture. Once in the correct position, he tried again. *"Boombastia!"* Fireworks shot out of the staff, exploding in a colorful display above!

Barley cheered. "You're a natural!" He ripped a chunk off the giant cheese puff and threw it at Ian. "Think fast!"

"Aloft Elevar!" said Ian, without missing a beat. Using magic, he caught it and tossed it back to Barley.

"Nice!" said Barley, popping the cheese-puff chunk into his mouth. He pulled an apple-sized piece off the boat and chomped down on it.

"Careful how much boat you're eating, there, man. We still gotta make it to the end of the tunnel," said Ian.

"Good point." Barley took another bite.

"I can't believe I'm *this close* to actually talking to Dad," said Ian.

"You know what I'm gonna ask him?" said Barley. "If he ever gave himself a wizard name."

"What?"

"Well, 'cause he was into magic. Lots of wizards have cool names: Alora the Majestic, Birdar the

Fanciful. Anyway, it'll just be nice to have more than four memories of him."

Ian turned to Barley. "Three. You only have three memories."

"Oh. Yeah."

"Barley, do you have another memory of Dad you haven't told me?" asked Ian, sensing his brother was hiding something.

Barley paused, a little pained. "It's . . . it's just not my favorite."

Ian asked him to explain. Barley glanced over at his brother and hesitated again. "When Dad was sick . . . I was supposed to go in and say goodbye to him. But he was hooked up to all these tubes, and . . . he just didn't look like himself. I got scared. And I didn't go in." Ian watched Barley's regretful expression as he thought about his words. "But that was when I decided I would never be scared again."

Ian gave his brother a soft smile. For the first time, he understood Barley's incredible fearlessness.

Just then, Barley noticed something ahead. Moments later, they stepped off the boat and climbed to an ornate ancient archway.

"The Final Gauntlet," said Barley in awe. "The Phoenix Gem is just on the other side."

Dad walked ahead of Ian on the leash. Barley spotted skeletons scattered about. "Careful, there could be booby traps."

"This place is, like, a thousand years old," said Ian. "There's no way there could be—"

At that moment, a blade swung from a hole in the wall, cutting off Dad's fake upper body and flinging it behind them! Barley and Ian gasped in horror.

A sudden wind picked up and blew out the torch. A trapdoor in the ceiling began to open, casting a sickly green light into the tunnel.

"Oh, no, it can't be . . . ," said Barley. A prickly rush of anxiety tingled through his body as something dropped from the ceiling. A green, jellylike cube jiggled toward them, engulfing Dad's fake upper body and instantly dissolving it! At the other end of the tunnel, a wall slowly lowered from the ceiling. If it reached the ground, it would lock them inside with the cube!

"Run!" yelled Barley.

Ian noticed a bunch of stones on the path ahead

that had symbols on them, and there were hundreds of holes in the walls.

"Wait!" he said. "It's some kind of puzzle. We gotta figure it out before we—"

"No time," interrupted Barley. "Grab a shield."

Barley and Ian frantically pried shields from the bony hands of nearby skeletons. Holding Dad protectively between them, they raced toward the opening beneath the descending wall. Barley screamed like a warrior while Ian screamed in panic. As they stepped on the marked stones, arrows and battle-axes released from the holes in the walls around them!

The cube continued to chase them, eating every weapon that shot into its path. Ian and Barley ran hard to make it under the wall—and stopped short when they found themselves at the edge of a drop. Razor-sharp spikes covered the bottom of a pit!

Ian turned to Barley. "Jump!" Barley looked at Ian like he was nuts.

"Trust me."

Barley glanced at the gelatinous monster behind them and the descending wall ahead. He closed his eyes . . . and jumped!

Ian conjured the Levitation Spell to stop Barley in midair! Then, dragging Dad along with him, Ian leapt off the edge and used Barley's head as a stepping-stone to get to the other side. Ian's magic lifted Barley over the rest of the pit just as the cube closed in.

Barley and Ian slid under the wall as it inched to the ground—but Dad was still on the other side! Ian tugged hard on the leash, pulling Dad under seconds before it slammed shut!

Ian took a step back, but Barley stopped him and pointed to a star-shaped tile on the ground.

"Don't step on that," warned Barley.

Suddenly, there was a clanging noise—it sounded like giant gears turning and shifting behind the walls. Then water rushed in, quickly lifting them off their feet and toward the ceiling!

"I didn't touch it!" exclaimed Ian.

As Barley tried to keep Dad afloat, Ian pointed the staff toward a hole in a round door at the top of the chamber.

"Voltar Thundasir!" Ian shouted. A lightning bolt shot out of the staff, but it bounced off the door. As they rose in the water, they could see that the hole was the same star shape as the tile on the ground.

"Maybe we were supposed to step on it?" said Barley.

Before Ian could stop him, Barley dove into the water. As Barley pressed on the tile with his foot, the door in the ceiling began to open! Ian cheered, but Barley couldn't hold his breath long enough to secure the door in place. The door closed as he swam back to the surface.

"It's impossible!" said Barley, gasping for air. "No one can hold their breath that long!"

Ian and Barley looked at each other and then at Dad, an idea striking them simultaneously. Ian held the leash and let Dad sink to the bottom. He guided Dad around, trying to get his feet to hit the tile. The water continued rushing in, rising higher and higher, threatening to submerge them.

Ian and Barley took their last gulp of air as the water line slipped over their heads. Just then, Dad stepped on the tile, and the door began to open again! Rays of light streamed in from above as the door locked into place!

The boys rose to the surface, inhaling great breaths of air as they climbed through the doorway. Laughing with relief, they pulled Dad up by the leash like fishermen reeling in a big catch.

"We made it!" said Barley.

Above them, they saw what looked like another portal. A short ladder embedded in the wall led right up to it.

"The Phoenix Gem awaits beyond this door! Shall we?" said Barley.

Ian smiled. "We certainly shall!"

They climbed the ladder, Ian in front, and laughed with anticipation and excitement.

"Dad, we have followed the quest, and it has led us to our victory!" announced Ian.

He anxiously pushed the panel aside and pulled himself up. He squinted as his eyes adjusted to the daylight. He couldn't believe what he saw.

Ian's smile dissolved as he realized where the long journey had taken them: to the middle of downtown New Mushroomton! His eyes darted around as they landed on each familiar landmark . . . the last one being his high school. He stared in disbelief. They were right back where they had started!

Barley climbed up beside him and looked around, just as shocked.

People walked around the square, bored and oblivious, like any other day. The boys peered out of a manhole in the street, wet, disheveled, and exhausted.

They wearily climbed out. A truck honked at them, and Barley pulled Ian and Dad out of the street.

"We're back home," said Ian.

"No, that doesn't make sense!" said Barley. "We

took the Path of Peril." He looked down at the wet, tattered kids' menu and the stone from the raven statue. "We followed the ravens, we went to the end of the water . . ." He looked more closely at the stone and mumbled, "Unless the X meant stay away from the water." He turned the stone, looking at the X another way. "Or it could be, like, a campfire. . . ."

Ian was crushed.

"It's okay," said Barley. "We can figure this out."

"Figure what out?" said Ian. "We're back where we started!"

"It has to be here. There was a gauntlet. I mean, unless that gauntlet was for, coincidentally, some different quest." He lowered his head. "That's a possibility. No, no, no, this has to be where the Phoenix Gem is. I followed my gut."

"Oh, no," said Ian. "The gem is in the mountain. The mountain we could have been to hours ago if we'd just . . . if we'd just stayed on the expressway."

"No, the expressway is too obvious, remember? You can never take the—"

"If I hadn't listened to you! Okay?" Ian interrupted, fuming. "I can't believe this. You act like you know what you're doing, but you don't have a clue . . . and that's because . . . you *are* a screwup! And now you have screwed up my chance to have the one thing I never had!"

Barley looked at Ian, hurt. Ian took Dad by the leash and started walking toward the park.

"Where are you going?" called Barley.

"To spend what little time we have left with Dad!" Ian looked at the staff in his hands with disgust and handed it to Barley.

Barley called after him. "We can still find the Phoenix Gem! We just have to keep looking!"

But Ian continued, ignoring his brother. As they walked through the park, Dad searched around with his foot.

"No, Dad. He's not here," said Ian, knowing he was looking for Barley.

Ian found a spot on a cliff and sat with Dad to watch the sun set over the ocean. It had been close to twenty-four hours since Ian had cast the Visitation Spell in his bedroom. He knew they were almost out of time.

Meanwhile, Barley frantically searched for another clue. "Come on, where is it?" He spotted the old fountain and gasped. "Follow the water!" He hurried toward it and jumped in. Onlookers pointed and whispered as he sloshed around in the dirty water.

Two construction workers approached. "All right, come on, out of the fountain," one said.

"No! I'm looking for an ancient gem!" cried Barley.

"Yeah, we know, the old days," said the other worker.

"No! Stop! Please! No!" begged Barley. The workers tried to pull him away and people passing by stopped to stare.

"Okay! Okay! Ow! Okay, I'm leaving!" said Barley, surrendering. Then he broke free and raced back into the water. They tried to grab him, but he climbed to the top of the fountain, wrapping his arms around its tall spire.

"Can someone call the cops?" said the worker. "We got the history buff again!"

Barley looked disheveled, desperate, and confused. Clinging to the fountain with the crowd staring at him, he suddenly felt like the screwup everyone had always believed him to be.

.⁺.✦.ᶜ☾ ✶⁺.⁺.

On the cliff, Ian sat with Dad watching the setting sun streak the sky with pinks and purples. Ian pulled out his list, heartbroken to miss the opportunity to do the things with Dad that he'd wanted to. He began to cross out each item. When he got to "driving lesson," he paused. He thought about how he had driven Guinevere when Barley was tiny. He remembered Barley instructing him and cheering him on. Ian knew it wasn't quite what he had expected when he'd written the list, but he placed a checkmark next to it.

Also on the list was "play catch." A memory of Barley throwing a piece of cheese puff and Ian catching it with magic came to mind. He gave it a check. Next he saw "laugh together." He recalled cracking up while dancing with Barley and Dad at the rest stop, and checked that one off, too.

Finally, he looked at the last item: "share my life with him." Ian's mind was flooded with memories of growing up with Barley. He could see them as kids playing in the pool together and having pillow fights. He remembered how Barley had taught him how to ride a bike. Barley always seemed to be there for him, cheering him on with confidence and pride.

Ian was surprised when he noticed he had checked off every item on his list. He smiled as tears welled up in his eyes. He folded the paper and put it in his pocket. Then he stood, took Dad by the leash, and raced off to find his big brother.

Barley was still on top of the fountain. Police officers called to him from below, but he refused to come down.

As he continued scanning for a clue, Barley noticed a clover shape on the fountain that matched the stone from the raven statue! He slowly pushed the stone into place. It fit perfectly, like the final piece of a puzzle.

Slowly, a chamber in the fountain opened to reveal . . . the sparkling Phoenix Gem!

Barley lit up with joy, laughing in disbelief. He grabbed the gem, not noticing the red, smoky mist rising out of the fountain.

Ian spotted Barley and ran toward him, calling out his name. Barley grinned at the sight of his brother and held up the Phoenix Gem.

Ian was thrilled until he saw the ominous red mist curling into the air. "Behind you!" he yelled.

Barley turned to see the mist waft past the shocked police officers. Suddenly, a realization dawned on him. "It's a curse!"

18

The red mist drifted across the street, forming a giant sphere in front of the high school. The sphere shot out tentaclelike arms that burst through the school, tearing through walls, lockers, and classrooms. It grabbed the debris and used it to form the armor of a terrible beast. It was a massive dragon!

Part of the gymnasium's wall depicting the school's goofy dragon mascot slid over to become the beast's face. It eyed the gem in Barley's hand and roared a terrifying garbled version of the school bell. Then it barreled toward Barley!

"Barley, RUN!" screamed Ian, hurrying to his brother.

Barley jumped down from the fountain, grabbed the staff, and took off. He called to the dragon. "What do you want? The gem?" He paused as he thought for a moment. "Fine. Take it!"

Ian was stunned as he watched his brother throw the gem as far as he could, sending the dragon racing after it.

Barley and Ian ran toward each other, and Barley revealed that he still had the real gem! He had tricked the dragon by throwing Guinevere's turn-signal light instead.

It didn't take long for the dragon to realize it had been fooled. It turned and breathed a path of fire between Barley and Ian so they were unable to reach each other. The dragon sprouted wings and took flight, then dove at Barley.

A dark shape suddenly swooped down from the sky with a mighty roar. The Manticore held the Curse Crusher high as she sliced the beast when she soared by, knocking it to the ground.

Barley cheered.

Ian squinted and saw someone riding on the Manticore's back. "Mom?"

Laurel stood atop the Manticore heroically. "It's okay, boys!" she called. "We'll take care of—"

Suddenly, the Manticore began to tip to one side.

"Whoa, you're tilting, you're tilting!" said Laurel, encouraging the Manticore to straighten out.

Ian called to his mother, worried, but she shouted, "Go see your father!"

"It's okay," Barley yelled to Ian. "If they stab the beast's core with that sword, the curse will be broken! Come on!"

Running up a hill, Ian dragged Dad on the leash as he hurried beside the fire path, trying to get to Barley. The dragon took off after the Manticore, giving chase over the cliffs and the ocean. The Manticore veered back toward land and dragged her sword along the ground, kicking up dirt into the dragon's eyes. She flew back around and sliced off one of the dragon's wings and then another.

In the meantime, the boys met at the top of the hill. Barley handed Ian the staff and placed the gem in its space at the top.

"Barley, about earlier, I am so sorry—" started Ian.

"There's no time!" said Barley. "The sun is about to set!"

They looked toward the lowering sun. It seemed to be sinking faster now. Ian wanted to say more, but he knew Barley was right. He held out the staff and recited, *"Only once is all we get; grant me this rebirth. Till tomorrow's sun has set, one day to walk the earth!"*

A bright beam of light shot from the staff. Ian held it with all his might, helping to make the magic work.

The Manticore flew toward the dragon, fast and fierce. "Time to crush a curse!"

She was about to deliver the killing blow when the dragon rose up and swatted the Manticore and Laurel out of the sky with its tail, sending them crashing to the ground!

Laurel got up, but the Manticore was unable to move. "Ooh, my back!" she screeched.

Determined, Laurel picked up the Curse Crusher. She saw the dragon turn its attention back to the boys and sprang into action. "I am a mighty warrior. . . ."

She climbed up the tail of the dragon. The music from her warrior workout video played in her mind as she used her moves to get closer and closer to the glowing core within the dragon's center.

The dragon reared up to attack the boys, and Laurel held the sword above her head with both hands. "I AM A MIGHTY WARRIOR!" she shouted.

She stabbed the dragon—but only part of the sword

made it past the armor into the beast's core. The boys watched as the dragon froze.

Laurel struggled to keep the sword in place. "Hurry! I can't hold this for long!" she yelled.

The gem slowly lifted out of the staff and spun. A warm light glowed around it and the staff began to shake, just as it did when Ian had conjured Dad in his bedroom.

"No, no, no, no, no—" Ian said, afraid he might lose his grip again. The magic swelled and was about to explode. "Barley!"

Barley ran over and braced his back against Ian's, giving him the support he needed. The gem rose over Dad and began raining powerful magic upon him, slowly building the rest of his body.

Just then, Laurel saw the dragon's armor begin to shift, slowly pushing the sword out of the core. The beast began to move again! It knocked Laurel down, flinging the sword into a pile of lockers.

"Boys! It's coming back!" she yelled.

The dragon locked its eyes on the gem. Ian and Barley watched, terrified that the dragon might get to the gem before Dad was complete!

Barley turned to Ian. "I'll go distract it!"

"What? No! If you do that, you'll miss Dad."

"It's okay. Say hi to Dad for me."

Ian knew what he had to do. "No. You go and say goodbye," he said firmly. He looked into Barley's eyes. "I had someone who looked out for me, someone who pushed me to be more than I ever thought I could be. I never had a dad . . . but I always had you."

Barley opened his mouth to respond, but before he could say anything, Ian grabbed the staff and sped off. He ran down the mountain and without hesitation, leapt off the edge, calling out the Trust Bridge Spell. *"Bridgrigar Invisia!"*

Glowing spots of light appeared under Ian's feet as he ran. When he approached the dragon, he cried, *"Boombastia!"* Fireworks shot from his staff, blinding the beast. It whipped its tail toward Ian as he shouted, *"Aloft Elevar!"* He stopped the tail with his magic.

Then suddenly, the dragon pulled its tail back in fury, sending Ian's staff sailing over the cliff and into the ocean. The Trust Bridge disappeared with the staff and Ian fell, cracking his ankle.

The dragon passed over Ian and marched straight toward Dad and Barley. "No. No. No. No!" shouted Ian.

Dad's body generated next to Barley as Barley fearfully counted the seconds, watching the beast move toward them.

"Use what I have," said Ian, remembering Barley's words. "What do I have? I have nothing!" He looked down at his empty hands. A splinter of wood from the staff had lodged itself into his skin. "Magic in every fiber . . ." He used his teeth to remove the tiny splinter and held it between his fingers. *"Magnora Gantuan!"* At his command, the splinter grew into a full-size staff!

Ian saw the dragon approach Barley and Dad, its mouth nearly on the gem. With every part of himself, Ian shouted, *"Voltar Thundasir!"*

BA-BAM!

A colossal bolt of white lightning shot from his staff and blasted the armor right off the dragon, knocking it to the ground. The dragon's weak spot was now exposed! Laurel finally reached the Curse Crusher and pulled it out of the pile of debris. She called to Ian and hurled the sword toward him.

"Accelior!" Ian shouted, catching it. The sword magically swung above his head, and just as the dragon began to rise, Ian sent the sword deep into its core!

The curse billowed into the air as an enormous cloud. Then it disappeared.

Ian fell to the ground, exhausted, surrounded by the rubble of the dragon's armor. The beast was gone. All was silent.

When Ian tried to stand, a sharp pain shot through his ankle. Then a warm burst of light came from the top of the hill. Ian limped as he carefully climbed up a pile of rubble, trying to get a view of Barley and Dad.

At the very top of the peak, Barley stood face to face with a glowing figure. The glowing subsided to reveal . . . Dad. Complete, from head to toe.

From his place in the rubble, Ian could only see Dad's back. He wished he could get closer, but he couldn't get through the debris with his injured ankle. He watched Dad and Barley talking and laughing together.

The sun sank below the horizon as Dad gave Barley a hug. Then, in an instant, he vanished in Barley's arms.

Barley quickly made his way toward Ian and helped him out of the rubble.

"What did he say?" Ian asked eagerly.

"He said he always thought his wizard name would be Wilden the Whimsical."

"Wow, that's really terrible," said Ian with a laugh.

"I know." Barley paused before continuing. "He also said he's very proud of the person you grew up to be."

"Well, I owe an awful lot of that to you," said Ian.

"He kinda said that, too," said Barley. "Oh, and he told me to give you this." Barley leaned down and gave Ian a huge, loving hug. And Ian didn't hold back as he hugged his big brother back with all his heart.

Epilogue

A while later, the Manticore stood in her tavern, which she had transformed back to how it looked in its glory days. The place continued to be very busy and welcomed anyone looking for adventure.

Dewdrop played darts with her fellow Pixie Dusters. She tossed a dart that started to drop toward the floor, but one of her friends swooped in, grabbed it, and flew it into the bull's-eye. "Ha, ha! Bull's-eye!" cheered Dewdrop.

The Manticore stretched out her wings as she spoke, entertaining a group of customers with one of her adventurous tales. She ignited candles on a cake with her fire breath and lifted the Curse Crusher above her head. "And then, with a slash of my mighty sword, I severed the beast's wings from its wretched body!" she said, bringing the sword down, splattering frosting everywhere.

She grinned. "Okay, who wants cake?"

There was a beat of silence before all the kids cheered. "YEAH!"

Their parents watched nervously as they wiped cake from their faces.

At the rebuilt high school, Ian stood in front of a classroom of his fellow students, wrapping up a presentation about magic. He held the wizard staff.

"And I think with a little bit of magic in your life . . . you can do almost anything," he said.

A student raised her hand. "Is that how you put the school back together?"

"Uh, yes!" answered Ian.

Another student interrupted. "Is that also how you destroyed the school in the first place?"

"Uh . . . also yes?" Ian admitted.

The bell rang and the class quickly dispersed. A group of students approached Ian as he collected his things.

"Hey, that was great," said Sadalia.

"You going to the park later?" asked a troll named Gurge.

"Yeah! See you there!" said Ian. Everyone waved as they parted ways.

Later, when Ian walked through the front door of his house, Blazey barreled around the corner and jumped on him, smothering him with kisses. He kneeled and wrestled with her.

Laurel hustled around the corner with the spray bottle. "Blazey! Down!"

"Who's a good dragon? Who's a good dragon?" Ian said to his pet.

"So, how was school?" asked Laurel.

"It was . . . really good," answered Ian.

"Well, all right," Laurel said, smiling proudly.

Just then, Colt came into the room and approached Ian. "Hey! There he is. You working hard?"

"Nope, hardly workin'," answered Ian. Colt let out a hearty laugh.

Laurel's phone buzzed as she got a text message. She checked her phone. "Oh, I gotta go. I'm meeting the Manticore for a night out." She grabbed a battle-ax.

Then Colt got a call on his police radio. He gave Laurel a kiss before quickly leaving.

"You forgot your keys!" Laurel called.

"Don't need 'em!" said Colt. "I was born to run. H'yah!" Colt's hooves clopped against the ground as he raced away.

Ian watched from the living room window as Colt galloped down the road, his mane flowing in the breeze.

Barley crept up behind Ian and put him in a headlock. In one swift move, Ian freed himself, slamming Barley to the floor. Barley smiled proudly.

Ian reached down and helped him up. "So, how's the new van?"

"Guinevere the Second is great. I've almost got enough saved up for a sweet paint job," said Barley.

"No . . . please don't," said Ian.

"Why not?"

Ian held up his staff and smiled. "Because I already took care of it."

He opened the garage to reveal the magical paint job he'd done on Barley's new van. In the art, a Pegasus carried Barley, as a warrior, with Ian, as a wizard, riding behind him.

Barley's eyes popped and he cheered. He absolutely loved it. "YEAH!"

They climbed into the new van, which had a license plate that read GWNIVER2. Barley backed it out of the garage and drove a little while before stopping at a fork in the road. The ramp to the expressway was to the left, and an old path was to the right.

"Okay, best way to the park is to take a little something called the Road of Ruin," said Barley.

"Mmm . . . too obvious," said Ian.

"Wait, what?"

"On a quest, the clear path is never the right one," said Ian.

Barley cheered as Ian raised his staff and cast a spell, magically lifting the van into the air! And with a crackle of magic, the brothers flew off toward the horizon.